TASTE

TEMPTATION SERIES, BOOK THREE

EVELYN BLOOM

EK PUBLISHING INC.

Edited by
L. Nunn Editing

Cover Art by
EK Designs

TASTE

Measure twice, bang once.

Building custom cabinets… easy.

Building a love life… who has time for that?

Busting his ass building his carpentry business, Connor Hayes jumps at the chance to construct a private library for millionaire book lover, Jack Walker. He can showcase his talents and boost his business, especially if Jack refers all of his rich friends.

There's only one problem: Connor's fierce obsession with Jack's sharp mind and his way too kissable mouth. Make that two problems…

Of all of Connor's bad ideas, sleeping with the customer when there's so much at stake is his worst.

But he can't get Jack out of his head.

Jack isn't relationship material. It doesn't matter how well Connor fills out a pair of jeans or how talented he is with his hands. He hired Connor to build his library, not fill the empty spot in his bed.

So, why is he finding odd jobs to keep Connor around?

And why does he find it increasingly difficult to keep his hands off Connor and not lose his heart in the process?

As Jack and Connor grow closer, they realize they have much in common. But that doesn't make things easy.

Can two people from opposite worlds find their happily ever after?

———

CHAPTER 1

Connor

"Are you fucking kidding me? Dude, you are killing me over here!" I could barely contain the urge to lay on the horn as the Cadillac in front of me slowed down to a near crawl. Gritting my teeth, I waited until the lane to my left had a big enough break in traffic for my rusty Silverado and zipped past the white Cadillac.

I checked the time, muttering another curse under my breath but resisting the temptation to speed. The last thing I could afford was a speeding ticket.

"It's fine, it's fine," I muttered as I took the exit for Abbotsdale. "You texted him and told him you were running late." I slowed my speed another twenty, keeping an eye out for kids in the affluent neighbourhood as I drove toward my new client's house.

Getting caught behind an accident today was the worst possible timing. While the traffic accident had been a simple fender bender, the combination of it plus rush hour traffic meant I was almost an hour late for my meeting with Jack

Walker. Collector of vintage cars and books, CEO of Walker Publishing House, and millionaire.

Hell, maybe even a billionaire.

Sweat was making my work shirt stick to my back, and I could feel it dripping down my temples. The air in my truck hadn't worked for years and while it was a pain in the ass in the summer, fixing the air conditioning in my vehicle was a luxury, not a necessity.

Of course, I regretted that decision as I pulled into the long circular driveway of Jack Walker's house and parked a little away from the front door.

"Mansion," I muttered. "The guy lives in a fucking mansion, not a house."

I stared at the sprawling rancher as I slid out of my truck and slammed the door shut. If Jack's home was less than six thousand square feet, I'd eat a fucking hardhat.

I glanced behind me at the quiet tree-lined street. The houses – excuse me, *mansions* - were far apart, not stuck together like the rowhouse I'd grown up in, where you heard every cough, sneeze, and fart from your neighbour.

Unease trickled into my belly as I studied the house across the street. Darryl lived in Abbotsdale now. His mother had run into our neighbour, Betty Simpson, at the grocery store not six months ago and gushed about Darryl's new place. Betty couldn't wait to share the news with me the next time she saw me at Ma's.

For all I knew, it could be Darryl's house I was looking at.

So what? Who cares? Darryl's been out of your life for years. Fuck that guy and his classist attitude.

I turned and headed toward the massive front doors. Rich people were all the same. Despite my brother Shepherd's obvious respect for his best customer, I wasn't hopeful that I'd like Jack Walker. There was no doubt in my mind that

Jack would look down his nose at me just like Darryl had learned to do. But since I'd be getting paid a lot of money to have Jack treat me like dirt, I'd swallow my pride and my temper and kiss the rich douchebag's ass all fucking day.

Rich folks knew other rich people, and if I could get in Jack's good graces, the odds of him recommending me to his millionaire friends was extremely high. A clientele of millionaires would not just build my carpentry business to the point where I could start marketing and maybe even hire an employee or two, but it would also give me the extra cash I needed to give my dream job a real shot.

I rang the doorbell and fanned my shirt, trying to cool myself down and regretting not carrying an extra shirt in my truck. I smelled my pits, hoping like fuck that my antiperspirant was still doing its job, and quickly lowered my arms when the door opened.

I stared at the man standing in the doorway, my throat drying up, my hand faltering, and my greeting dying on my lips.

Fuck me. Please don't let this be Jack Walker.

The man wearing the dark suit with a blood red tie and light grey shirt was beautiful. Not attractive. Not handsome. No, he was beautiful, and I would have been perfectly happy to stand in the doorway and stare at his gorgeous hazel eyes until time simply ended.

He arched one brow before holding his hand out. "Connor Hayes? I'm Jack Walker."

Fuck me *sideways.*

I cleared my throat and wiped my sweaty palm on the thigh of my chinos before shaking his hand. "Hello, Mr. Walker. I'm sorry again about being late."

"It's not a problem. I had a meeting that ran a bit late as well. Come inside."

I followed him in, studying the interior of his home with what I hoped looked like polite interest and not drooling envy. The rancher had an open concept with a wide hallway on either end of the combined living room/kitchen area.

The far wall was a combination of floor-to-ceiling windows and two sets of patio doors on either end that opened into the backyard. A crystal clear inground pool, surrounding deck, and small pool house took up a fair amount of space, but there was still plenty of lush green grass and even a small grove of what looked like apple trees at the far end of the fenced-in property.

The kitchen was a sleek and shiny design of white cupboards, quartz countertops, and stainless-steel appliances. The large island provided plenty of space to eat for at least six people. The living area was separated by a floor-to-ceiling partition that featured a large gas fireplace, and a flat screen television mounted just above the fireplace. A grey sectional sofa and round glass coffee table finished the look.

The lack of clutter made my minimalist heart happy. After growing up with five siblings in a small and cramped three-bedroom rowhouse, where I was constantly tripping over another human or a mountain of their stuff, I craved the vast open space of a home like this with minimal décor.

Jack was standing patiently beside me as I took in his home. "You have a beautiful home, Mr. Walker."

"Thank you. I was at your brother's garage earlier today and mentioned we were meeting this afternoon," Jack said. "He had nothing but good things to say about your work."

"Well, he's my brother, so this is the part where I tell you to take everything he says about me with a grain of salt."

"But?" Jack asked when I didn't say anything else.

"But he is one hundred percent accurate about my work."

Jack laughed, and my dick immediately sat up and

considered saying hello. I gritted my teeth and focused on the crown molding along the wall. "The crown molding is incredible."

"Is it?" Jack said. "I'll confess that I wouldn't know the difference between good crown molding and bad crown molding. But my interior designer insisted that it was needed to 'bring the room together'."

"It's a good choice," I said.

Jack slipped out of his suit jacket and draped it over the couch. "Thank you. So, the library is down this hallway."

I slipped cloth booties over my shoes before following Jack down the hallway.

"This side of the house has my office, the library, a guest bedroom, and full guest bathroom," Jack said as we walked to the double doors at the end of the hallway. I studied his perfect ass and thick thighs, doing my best not to imagine what that perfect ass might look like naked and failing miserably.

Jack opened the doors and I followed him in, whistling under my breath at the size of the room. Like the rest of the house, the far wall housed floor-to-ceiling windows. One wall had a gas fireplace, and the walls were painted a rich dark blue that helped give the enormous room a warm and cozy feeling.

A sleek and modern grey desk sat in the middle of the room, and two grey wingback chairs were in the far corner, but the rest of the library was bare, with not even a single book in sight.

"This is a good size room," I said, and then had to stifle my laughter. Jack's library alone was bigger than my entire apartment.

Jack ran his hand along the top of the desk. "I have a lot of books - close to ten thousand. Building a library in my home has been a dream of mine since I was a child. Now that I finally have the chance to do it, I want it to be perfect."

"What type of shelving are you looking for?" I asked. I tried not to look like I was dying to blurt out my ideas, but they were flowing into my head fast and furious.

Jack studied me for a moment. "If this was your library you were building, what would you do to this room?"

It was a test. Jack's way of finding out if I would slap a couple of bookshelves up against a wall and call it a day, or if I would be an eager participant in helping his childhood dream come true. A test that, if I failed, would mean the potential closure of my business. I took a deep breath. I could do this.

CHAPTER 2

Jack

I was in trouble. Not, *my newest author is failing* trouble, but *I really want to fuck the obviously straight carpenter* trouble.

I tried not to stare at the way Connor's shirt stretched to accommodate his broad shoulders or place a bet in my head on when exactly his sleeves would just rip open, thanks to the immense pressure from his large biceps.

Focus!

Right, focus.

"Obviously, I'd do floor to ceiling bookshelves," Connor said. "Two rolling ladders to make the top shelves accessible, and I'd make the shelves a bit deeper than standard, say thirteen inches instead of twelve."

Did Connor have twelve inches? Fuck, I'd sell half my damn company to find out.

"The room is big enough that it wouldn't feel crowded even with bookshelves that deep on each wall." Connor was starting to walk around the room, studying each wall and eyeing the wingbacks at the far end. "Based on what I've seen of the house, I'd carry the minimalist theme into the library as well. Sleek shelving with clean lines and building them from hardwood will solve any potential sag issues with the shelves. Although it would be more expensive to go with hardwood."

He glanced over at me, and I said, "Cost is not an issue."

I followed him across the room – my God, the man's ass was a work of *art* – stopping when he did a few feet from the windows along the back wall. Pure child-like excitement crossed his face, and the enthusiasm in his voice made me grin.

"What would be really cool is a reading nook. I could create one using pillars of shelving to enclose in this area in front of the window. The pillars would come out to, say about here, leaving an entrance into the reading area. The pillars would be open on two sides, so almost like two bookshelves back to back, but prettier, you know?"

He glanced at me, and my cock twitched at the grin on his face and the way his dark brown eyes had lit up with excitement. Fuck, he really was gorgeous. But I had a foolproof gaydar, and the gorgeous man standing in front of me didn't set off a single ping.

"That sounds good," I said.

"Oh, and I could build a curved shelf that rested on top of the bookshelves to section the reading nook off, basically make it into its own small room within the library, as well as give you more bookshelf space. You could add a couple of lamps, hang a few pieces of book related art on the walls, maybe even a small coffee table. I have a small modern one that would fit perfectly in here."

"You sell coffee tables?" I asked.

A bit of colour rose in his cheeks, and he cleared his

throat. "Oh, uh, I have a small side hustle selling furniture I've made."

Before I could reply, he said, "Sorry, am I overstepping here with my ideas? I feel like maybe I got a little carried away. Obviously, I'm a carpenter, not an interior designer, and I'm aware that my job is to build the look you and your designer create, not put my own spin on it. I promise if you hire me, I'll make exactly what you're asking me to make."

"I asked for your opinion," I said. "I love all of your ideas for my library and look forward to seeing the final vision. That is, if you want to work on the project and can fit it into your schedule in the next month or two. I'd like to finish it sooner rather than later, but your brother did mention that your schedule is often full."

He jerked a little, his eyes widening in surprise and a pleased grin crossing his face. "Thank you. I absolutely want to work on this project. I could start it next week if that works for you?"

Now it was my turn to twitch in surprise. "Sure. That would be great, actually."

"Perfect. Tuesday morning, I'll take some measurements and give you a cost estimate for supplies. In the meantime, I'll write up the contract and email it to you. Take a look at it, and if you have any questions, we can discuss them on Tuesday."

"Sure," I said.

"You work from home most days?" Connor said.

I nodded. "Usually three days here and two days in the office downtown."

"I'll try to keep noise to a minimum but with your home office so close to the library…"

"It won't be a problem," I said. "Either I'll go to the

downtown office, or I'll work in my bedroom on the other side of the house."

"Great." Connor left the library. Ignoring my urge to find another reason to keep him here, I walked him to the front door.

He held out his hand and I shook it, the dry rasp of his palm sending pleasant shivers up and down my back. "I'm looking forward to working with you, Mr. Walker."

"Call me Jack," I said.

"Jack," he said. "It was nice to meet you."

"You too, Connor." I was still holding his hand, and when Connor glanced at our clasped hands, I immediately dropped his hand, my cheeks hot and cursing myself inwardly.

The door opened, and Mark walked in. My best friend paused with his hand on the doorknob, smiling uncertainly at us. "Oh, sorry. I didn't mean to interrupt."

"No worries," I said as Mark closed the door. "Mark, this is Connor. He'll be working on my library. Connor, this is my best friend, Mark."

"Nice to meet you." Mark shook Connor's hand.

Connor studied him for a moment before recognition and excitement flashed across his face. "Holy shit! You're Mark Reynolds. You write the Shadow Wood series. I've read all eleven books in the series."

He was still holding Mark's hand, and he pumped it enthusiastically. "You're a great writer, man. Sincerely. My sister and I are big fans. She'll be so jealous when she finds out I've met you."

Mark grinned at him. "Thanks, Connor. I appreciate the support, and I'm glad you like the books."

"Not just like, love," Connor said. He realized he was still holding Mark's hand and dropped it as a dull flush filled his cheeks. "We're so stoked about book twelve. Nora and I have already pre-ordered our copies."

"That's great," Mark said. "Once you have them, let Jack know, and I'll be happy to sign them if you'd like."

The grin that crossed Connor's face made me want to do something stupid, like pushing him up against the wall and kissing him.

"That would be awesome. Thanks, man. It was really great to meet you." He shook Mark's hand again before opening the door and glancing at me. "I'll have the contract emailed to you by tomorrow. Have a great day."

"You as well," I said, then watched the finest ass I'd ever seen leave my house.

When the door closed, Mark grinned at me. "You're drooling."

"Did you see that perfect ass on that perfect straight man?"

Mark laughed. "It was a great ass. Sorry again to interrupt your potential new hook-up."

"You weren't interrupting. Didn't you hear me? He's straight."

"You don't know that for sure."

"Yeah, I do," I said. "My gaydar is never wrong. Remember? Besides, his brother's gay. What are the odds of two brothers in the same family being gay?"

"There isn't some rule where only one member of the family is allowed to be gay," Mark said as he followed me toward the kitchen. "My cousin and I are both gay."

"Yeah, but your brother is straight as an arrow." I opened the fridge. "You want a beer before I start grilling?"

"Sure." Mark took the offered beer and twisted open the cap. "Again, there's no rule about how many gay people can be in one family."

I just shrugged before taking a sip of my beer. "How did your day go?"

Mark grimaced. "Long. I wanted to get at least five thousand words today but was so fucking tired that I couldn't concentrate."

"You do look a little sleep deprived," I said, as I took the steaks out of the fridge and set them on the island.

"You would too, if you were kept awake by loud and terrible music for half the fucking night," Mark grumbled.

"I take it you haven't solved the issue of your hard-partying neighbour," I said.

Mark shook his head. "The asshole won't even come to the door when I knock."

"Why not call the cops?"

"Because I don't want to be that guy," Mark said. "He's young, at least I think he is – and I don't want to be the old guy next door making noise complaints."

"Old guy?" I said. "You're forty-two, Mark. That's not old."

"It is to my neighbour. He's maybe twenty-five... maybe."

I shrugged. "I'm sure it's bothering the other neighbours, so even if you did call the cops, the guy wouldn't know for sure that it's you."

"Walter on the other side is eighty-seven and almost completely deaf," Mark said. "And Corey and Melissa across the street are in Europe for the next two months."

I picked up the steaks, and Mark followed me out onto the patio. I pointed to one of the loungers next to the pool. "Have a seat while I get the steaks started."

When I returned, Mark had stripped off his shirt and was sprawled on the lounger with his eyes closed, soaking in the late afternoon sun. I studied his body as I sat in the lounger beside his. Despite how often he grumbled about his age, Mark had a fantastic body. He might have been seven years older than me, but his abs were more defined than mine, and I'd seen him bench press two-fifty without breaking a sweat.

"Why are you staring at me, creeper?" Mark said without opening his eyes.

I laughed and took a sip of my beer. "Sorry, I was just thinking that for an *old man*, you have one hell of a body."

He grunted in thanks. "How did your third date with that lawyer go?"

"Fine."

"Fine?" Mark took a drink of beer. "Considering the third date is the 'fuck' date, fine isn't promising."

"We didn't fuck," I said. "I broke it off with him. He wasn't my type."

"Meaning what?"

"He was boring," I said. "The only books he reads are law textbooks, and he doesn't even own a car. He takes transit everywhere, for God's sake. Says driving makes him nervous."

"Well, you wouldn't have to worry about him taking one of your cars for a joyride," Mark said with a grin.

I got up to flip the steaks, and Mark followed me, sinking into one of the chairs next to the patio table. "This is the fourth guy you've gone out with who's either a lawyer or a doctor. You could expand your dating search from the exciting world of law and medicine, you know."

"That's not true," I said. "I asked out the mechanic from Shepherd's shop."

"You did," Mark said. "And if he'd agreed to go out with you, you would have done what you always do."

"What's that supposed to mean?" I glared at him as I flipped the steaks and closed the lid to the barbeque.

"It means that a mechanic, especially an apprentice, doesn't make that much money. Since you only date guys who have an equal amount of, or more money than you, the mechanic would have been one of your fuck 'em once and then say goodbye flings."

I wanted to argue. Instead, I took a long swallow of beer. Mark was right. I'd had no intention of doing anything with Tristan other than taking him to my bed once or twice. Of course, considering that the shop owner, Shepherd, had a thing for Tristan and almost dropped me as a client from his shop, it was a good thing Tristan turned me down flat. A good mechanic is worth way more to me than a one-night stand. And Shepherd is the best mechanic in town.

Mark was studying me over the rim of his beer bottle. I sighed and said, "Yeah, you're right."

"You know that not every blue-collar guy you meet is after your money, right?" Mark said. "Justin was the exception, not the rule."

"Maybe, maybe not," I said.

"But you're not willing to ever find out," Mark said.

"No need," I said. "The right guy in my tax bracket is out there. I just need to find him."

Mark burst into laughter. "Your tax bracket? Dude, you so need therapy."

"Everyone needs therapy," I said.

"True." The smile faded from his face. "Seriously, Jack. You deserve to be happy after what Justin did to you."

I shrugged. "I'm not the first rich guy to be fooled by a grifter, and I won't be the last. But I've learned my lesson, and I know better now."

"Which means you don't have to limit your dating pool to boring lawyers and asshole doctors," Mark said. "You can date someone you're interested in for reasons other than they want or need your vast wealth."

I laughed. "Vast wealth? Take it down a notch, buddy."

"Says the billionaire."

"Millionaire."

"Multi-millionaire."

"Fine, I'm loaded," I said. "But it's not like you're doing so terrible yourself. You're at the top of my midlist authors. Six figures a year isn't anything to turn your nose up at."

"I do all right for myself," Mark said with a modest grin. "Anyway, my point is, I know you've been burned in the past, and I get that you're a bit cautious, but you still shouldn't limit yourself like this. It's just dating, right? And if it turns into something more... permanent, that's what prenups are for."

"That's romantic," I said with a grimace.

"Do you want romance, or do you want to make sure they love you for more than your money?"

"I want both," I said.

"Then, buddy," Mark said with a solemn tip of his beer bottle to me, "I hate to say it, but you need to do something about your trust issues."

CHAPTER 3

Connor

"Wait, you met *the* Mark Reynolds? Are you shitting me right now?"

"Nora," James glared at our sister before glancing at Eva sitting beside him, "language. How many times have I asked you not to curse in front of my kid?"

"Whoops. Sorry, Eva." Nora dug into her pocket, produced a dollar, and handed it across the table to Eva.

Eva stuffed it into the front pocket of her overalls before slurping up a spaghetti noodle. "It's fine, Daddy. Uncle Connor swears in front of me all the time."

"Hey, nobody likes a narc, kid," I said.

Eva grinned at me, a ring of tomato sauce around her mouth before slurping up another noodle.

"Eva, chew your noodles instead of slurping, please," James said. "It's bad manners to slurp."

"Shepherd, honey, can you pass me the garlic bread?" My mother gave my oldest brother an affectionate look.

"Who's Mark Reynolds?" Shepherd's boyfriend, Tristan, asked.

"Who's Mark Reynolds? *Who's Mark Reynolds?*" Nora looked like she was about to have a stroke. "Only the best fu-freaking author in the world, that's who."

Shepherd finished his last bite of spaghetti before leaning back and resting his arm along the back of Tristan's chair. "He's a local suspense author. Connor and Nora are obsessed with him. He writes this series, Shadow Falls."

"Shadow *Wood*," Nora said. "He's so amazing, Tristan. I'll lend you the first book in the series if you want to read it."

"Sure," Tristan said. "I'm always looking for new authors to read."

Nan was sitting at the head of the table between Shepherd and me. She took my hand and smiled at me as Eva said, "January fourth is National Spaghetti Day."

"How do you know that?" James said.

"I read it in a book," Eva said.

"Speaking of books," Nan said, "how did your interview go today with Shepherd's client, Connor?"

"Good," I said. "He offered me the job."

"That's wonderful," Nan squeezed my hand again as James punched me in the arm, and Ma clapped her hands.

"I'm so proud of you, honey," Ma said.

"Thanks, Ma. You should see this guy's house. You'd love it."

"The guy is richer than God," Shepherd said. "Last I counted, he has fourteen vintage or rare cars."

James whistled under his breath. "What the hell does a guy do with fourteen cars?"

"Where does he keep the cars?" I said to Shepherd. "He's only got a three-car garage at the house."

"Only," Nora said with a laugh. "Ah, to be that rich."

"He had a garage built to store them, a few miles from his place," Shepherd said. "I've been there a couple of times. It's temperature controlled, and it has so many alarms, you'd think he stored the fucking Mona Lisa in it."

Eva held out her hand and grinned at Shepherd. Grimacing, he dug his wallet out of his back pocket and handed over a dollar bill. She stuffed it into her overalls pocket with the other one and grinned at Nan. "When I'm older, I'm gonna have fourteen cars too, all of them the Ford Mustang Shelby GT500, just in different colours."

"That sounds lovely, dearest," Nan said. "Although perhaps a bit expensive."

Eva shrugged. "I'm gonna be rich when I grow up. I'm gonna be a mechanic like Uncle Shepherd and a ballet dancer like Auntie Nora."

"Neither of them is rich." Davey, our youngest brother, walked into the kitchen. He held a basketball in one hand, and he dropped a kiss on Ma's cheek. 'Sorry I'm late, Ma. The game ran long."

"That's fine. I set a plate in the microwave for you," Ma said.

"Uncle Shepherd's rich," Eva said as Davey heated his plate of spaghetti. "He has a motorcycle and a car."

"That doesn't make someone rich, kiddo," Davey said. "You need to be a doctor or a lawyer if you want to make serious quid."

Eva scowled at her empty plate of spaghetti. "I wish I could get paid to read."

James laughed and kissed the top of her head. "Don't we all, Bunnykins. C'mon, let's get you into the tub... you've got spaghetti sauce in your hair."

James and Eva left, and the minute they were out of the

room, Nora grinned at me. "So, is Jack as hot as Tristan said he is?"

"Didn't notice," I said.

Shepherd grunted in annoyance. "You told her Jack was hot?"

Tristan grinned at him. "You know he is, honey." He leaned over and pressed a kiss against Shepherd's mouth. "But you're way hotter."

"You two are so cute," Nora said.

"So gross," I said.

Shepherd flipped me the bird before giving Tristan that starry-eyed, *I'm so in love with this man*, that actually *was* kind of cute. I'd never seen Shepherd this head over heels over a guy before, and I was both happy for him and jealous. Over the last couple of years, I'd barely had time for the occasional hook-up, let alone an actual relationship. It turns out, trying to build a company from the ground up, took a lot of fucking time and effort.

"Speaking of cute," Ma said, "I met the nicest young man at the grocery store yesterday. I showed him a picture of you, honey, and he gave me his number, said to text him if you were interested in having coffee. He was very handsome."

"Ma," I groaned, "you have to stop talking to random strangers at the grocery store. Seriously."

She shrugged. "I can't help it if I have a friendly face that just screams, 'ask me about produce.' People are always chatting with me at the grocery store. Anyway, I'll text you his number. You should call him. His name is Rick, and he's in finance. His suit was very," she paused and said delicately, "expensive looking."

"Not interested," I said.

Ma's look was sympathetic, but Nan said bluntly, "Not every rich guy is a dickhead, dearest."

Tristan's mouth dropped. He hadn't been dating Shepherd long enough to know that Nan had a mouth as filthy as the rest of us. She just hid it better.

"I know that, Nan," I said.

"Do you? Because Darryl didn't become an asshole once he made all his money. He was always an asshole." She smiled serenely at me as Tristan choked on his swallow of water. Shepherd thumped him on the back, and Ma handed him another napkin.

"So, Davey, how's the college application process going?" I said in a blatant effort to change the subject.

Nan, her eyes filled with the same warm love I'd seen since I was a young boy, squeezed my hand again and let the subject drop.

"I LOVE ALL OF IT." JACK SCANNED THE SKETCHES I'D LAID out on the island. He was dressed casually today in a polo shirt and a pair of jeans that probably cost more than my entire wardrobe. They also showed off his beautiful ass in a way that made my dick very happy.

"I can make changes to anything you want," I said. "The bookshelf arch leading into the reading area could be -"

"No," Jack said as he leaned over the island to take a closer look at a section of the sketch.

I stared at his ass as the front of my jeans grew tight. Christ, popping a fucking boner in front of my new client was a damn fine way to get fired.

"It's perfect exactly as it is."

"Yeah, perfect," I mumbled, my eyes still glued to Jack's butt as I pressed up against the island to hide my growing stiffy.

I looked away just as Jack glanced over at me, sweat sliding down my back despite the central air and my heart thumping like a rabbit. I knew Jack was gay, but it didn't mean he would appreciate me staring at his ass.

"So, I received the signed contract this morning, and with your approval of the sketches, I can pick up the supplies and get started tomorrow," I said.

I could see the surprise on his face, and I cleared my throat. "If that works with your schedule."

"It does," he said. "I've just never had a contractor be so... prompt in starting a job."

"I guess I'm a different kind of contractor," I said. I didn't think he needed to know that I was determined to do a perfect job in the hopes that he would recommend me to his rich friends.

"I guess you are." Jack's gaze slipped to my mouth and lingered.

New awareness tingled down my body and straight to my dick. Holy fuck, Jack was attracted to me. My dick practically screamed hallelujah, but my brain sent out immediate warning signals. I might have been hot for Jack, but forgetting that he was my new client, and this job was my one chance to expand my business, dating a rich guy was number one on my *never do that again* list.

Well, you're pretty fucking full of yourself, aren't you? If Jack is attracted to you, he's looking for nothing but a quick fuck. Don't fool yourself into thinking it's anything more than that.

My inner voice was right. Guys like Jack didn't date guys like me. Darryl had made that perfectly clear.

Jack was still staring at my mouth and hadn't even noticed the awkward silence that was starting. Trying like hell to ignore the half a stiffy I was sprouting, I said, "Okay, well,

I'll make a list of supplies and give you a cost estimate before I purchase them."

"No need," Jack said. "Just buy what you need and don't worry about the cost." He paused, his gaze returning to mine. "Do you need me to purchase the supplies?"

I wondered if he could see the offense on my face. Not that there was even a point in being offended. Of course he would think that I couldn't afford them or my credit wasn't good enough. It was the way guys like him thought. I shouldn't take it personally.

"No need, Mr. Walker," I said, my voice curt. "I'll invoice you for the cost once the job is finished."

"Right, of course." The embarrassment in Jack's voice and the muscle ticking in his temple let me know I'd done a piss poor job of disguising my offense.

I gathered the sketches into a neat pile as Jack said, "Before you go, could we discuss the coffee table you mentioned at our initial meeting?"

"Sure." I did a better job at hiding my surprise.

"Do you have any pictures of it?"

I opened my phone and scrolled to the folder of my furniture. I found the picture and gritted my teeth when Jack moved closer, and our shoulders brushed. Willing my fucking cock to behave, I said, "I think this one would go great in the room. It has a modern design and is made from the same hardwood I'll be using for the bookshelves."

Jack studied it before nodding. "I agree. I'll take it. How much?"

"Three fifty," I said, hoping the absolute glee in my voice couldn't be heard.

"Email me an invoice for it, and I'll have my accountant e-transfer the amount to you this afternoon," he said. "Would you mind if I took a look at some of your other pieces?"

"Oh, uh, sure." There was no hope of hiding my shock this time.

With a bemused smile on his face, Jack scrolled through the pictures, stopping to study an elaborately carved headboard that had taken me nearly nine months to finish.

"This is incredible. Did you do all the carving work yourself?"

I nodded. "By hand."

"Holy shit. How long did that take?"

"Nine months," I said.

"Incredible," he murmured before scrolling through more pictures. He stopped on a matching set of nightstands, studying them thoughtfully. "I'd be interested in these as well. What's the price of these?"

Excitement brewing in my belly, I leaned in to get a closer look at which ones he was looking at. "Eight hundred for the pair."

Jack didn't reply, and I turned my head, my breath catching in my throat at how close our faces were now. Close enough that I could see the tiny flecks of brown in the hazel of his irises, close enough that I could smell the sweet mint of his breath, close enough that I could kiss those full lips.

His voice husky, his gaze on my mouth, Jack said, "Maybe I could take a look at them in person? If you give me your address, I could drop by later tonight."

Common sense screamed to life. I moved further down the island, breaking the connection between us and managing to keep my raging erection hidden by staying pressed up against the island.

"They're, uh, not at my place," I said. "I rent a storage unit for the furniture I make. But I can meet you there one evening or load the nightstands into the truck and bring them by if that's easier."

Jack's cheeks were flushed, and he didn't exactly meet my gaze as he set my phone down on the island. "Whichever is easiest for you."

My damn cock had finally gone down, but my lust for Jack was still waving its fucking hand around like an overeager student. I needed to get the fuck out of here before I did something foolish, like trying to kiss my new client.

I picked up my phone and the sketches. "Okay, great. I'll, uh, get back to you on that. I need to go, but I'll be back tomorrow. I'll need a place to set up my table saw and other equipment. Is your preference the front or back of the house?"

"Back of the house, please," Jack said as he studied a spot over my left shoulder. "I have some neighbours who are bound to complain to the homeowner's association about the," he made quote marks with his fingers, "mess."

Of course, they would. And I knew exactly what Jack meant by mess. Rich people preferred that people like me stayed the fuck out of their neighbourhood. Irritated, I turned and practically stomped toward the door. Without looking in Jack's direction, I called, "See you tomorrow, Mr. Walker," and left, barely managing not to slam the door behind me like a pissed-off toddler.

CHAPTER 4

Jack

My lungs screaming at me, I did one final lap in the pool before clinging to the side of it and wiping the salt water from my face. I boosted myself out and sat on the side, my feet dangling in the water as I reached for the towel I'd left close to the diving board.

I dried my face and hair but let the evening sun and slight breeze dry the water on my upper body. Even with the breeze, the heat was still oppressive, but I didn't move into the shade. I stared into the crystal clear water, my thoughts jumbled and my stomach still in knots.

I'd fucked up. It was such a fucking cliché for the gay man to hit on the straight guy, and I'd been sick to my stomach since Connor had practically run out of my house this morning. I muttered a curse before standing and drying my legs. I wrapped the towel around my waist and headed to the outdoor kitchen at the far end of the patio. I grabbed a beer, twisted it open, and drank half of it.

I checked my phone that I'd left lying on the table. Mark

had replied to my text, but he was having dinner with friends and couldn't come over. I sent back a brief reply and considered texting Kurt or Adam before setting my phone down.

I liked Kurt and Adam, but I wasn't close to them the way I was close to Mark. Even just the idea of telling them that I had hit on a straight man made me shudder, and fresh embarrassment flooded through me.

I sighed and drank some more beer, staring at my phone. I wasn't a man who got lonely very often, but I couldn't deny that's what I was feeling. I was an only child, and my mom had died when I was twelve. My father raised me on his own, and we'd had a great relationship.

Joining him at the publishing company he'd started nearly twenty years before had been a no brainer. The pride in his voice and his face when I'd help turn it around from the verge of bankruptcy to a thriving multi-million-dollar company was one of the most defining moments of my life.

His death from pancreatic cancer four years ago was a devastating blow, and if it hadn't been for Mark, I don't know what I would have done. Another wave of loneliness washed over me, but I ignored it grimly. I couldn't do anything about the loneliness, but I could do something about the sick feeling in my stomach. I knew what I needed to do, but, fuck, did I wish I could just pretend this morning had never happened.

"For fuck's sake," I muttered. "Just do it before you get the damn text from Connor saying he's changed his mind about building the library. You're fucking lucky it hasn't happened already."

I snatched up my phone and scrolled to Connor's name in my contacts. Before I could lose my nerve, I typed out a quick text.

Connor, I'd like to apologize for earlier today when I

*made you uncomfortable. I can assure you that it will not
happen again.*

I pressed send before I could add anything else. There
was nothing else I could say. I just had to hope that my
apology was enough. I stared at the screen, but no three dots
indicated that Connor was replying.

I set my phone face down on my table and drank some
more beer, slapping at the occasional mosquito as I stared at
the apple tree at the far end of the property. There was a thick
branch just perfect for hanging a swing. Someday, I hoped to
have my kid swinging happily from that tree branch, but I
was already thirty-five, and I hadn't even had sex in six
months, let alone found the man of my dreams.

Shit, the self-pity was strong with me tonight. I needed to
finish my beer, have a cold shower, and go to bed early. I had
a long day tomorrow, and after Connor arrived, I'd be
heading to the office until at least eight. I needed all the rest I
could –

My phone dinged, and I nearly dropped my beer, scram-
bling to grab it. I flipped it over, my stomach flipping right
along with it when I saw Connor's name.

No problem. See you tomorrow.

My body deflated. I read the brief message twice more
then finished off the last of my beer. Leaving the bottle on the
table, I headed for the shower, dropping my phone on the bed
before stripping off my wet suit and tossing it into the
hamper.

I don't know why I was so disappointed. I should have
been happy that Connor didn't seem upset by the way I'd
nearly fucking kissed him in my kitchen this morning.
Instead, I wished that he'd made me work for the apology a
little harder, if only so I'd have an excuse to keep talking
to him.

Shaking my head at how stupid I was, I turned on the shower and stepped inside, ducking my head under the hot water to wash the salt away, wishing I could wash away the thoughts of Connor as easily.

Connor

I CLIMBED INTO MY TRUCK, TOSSED THE BAG ONTO THE passenger seat, and slammed the door shut before starting it. My shirt stuck to my back with sweat, and the heat in the truck was stifling despite my only being in the store for fifteen minutes. I wished again that I had the funds to fix the damn air conditioning. I rolled down the window and drove out of the Home Depot parking lot, turning left on Maple and heading back toward Jack's place.

I really needed to talk to Jack about looking at the night-stands. If he bought them, I could use the money to fix the a/c in the truck. Of course, I'd have to see Jack to talk to him. In the last week and a half, I'd seen him exactly once, the morning I started the job.

He'd given me a key to his house, told me to help myself to the cold drinks in the fridge, and headed out the door. I hadn't seen him since. We'd texted a few times, just progress reports on my part, and a few compliments about the progress of the bookshelves on his part, but there'd been no actual sightings of him or his very biteable ass.

After I'd nearly kissed him in his kitchen, I knew it was for the best, so why was I so annoyed that he was very obviously avoiding me? I didn't want to date him, so what did it matter if I never saw his perfect mouth or gorgeous body again?

Maybe you don't want to date him, but you could at least think about fucking him.

I ignored my inner voice and the way it was pouting like a spoiled teenager. A casual fuck with Jack might be precisely what my dick wanted, but it was madness to even think about it. I didn't know how many fucking times I had to tell myself he was my client, and I absolutely could not sleep with him, but I was pretty sure I was up to about four thousand times at this point.

My phone buzzed as I stopped for a red light. I hit the speaker button. "Hey, James. What's up?"

"Connor, are you still at work?" James's voice was frantic, and the hair on the back of my neck immediately stood up.

"What's wrong?" I said. "Who's hurt?"

The memory of calling Shepherd, of having to be the one to tell him that Dad was dead, washed over me like it was yesterday and not eighteen years ago.

"Everyone's fine," James said quickly. "Sorry, I didn't mean to freak you out."

I sucked in a deep breath as the light turned green, and I stepped on the gas. "It's okay. What's wrong?"

"I'm stuck at work. My fucking asshole of a co-worker screwed up an account, and I have to fix it before the client goes apeshit. Eva needs to be picked up at school, and Mom is at a doctor's appointment with Nan, Davey has a migraine, Angie's showing a client a house, and Shepherd's not answering his phone."

"Nora's off work today," I said. "Did you ask her?"

"I did, but she just ate a couple of gummy edibles and is too high to drive."

"Okay," I said. "I'll swing by the school and pick up Eva."

"Thanks, buddy, I owe you," James said. "I'll let the school know you're picking her up today."

"I'll have to take her to the job site with me. Building the library is a massive job, and I can't afford to lose any time on it."

"I get it, and that's not a problem at all. Eva always has a book in her backpack, so just set her up in a quiet corner with it. Honestly, I should be done here in the next hour and a half. Text me Jack's address, and I'll pick her up as soon as I'm done."

"Sounds good. Talk to you later," I said.

"Thanks again, Connor. Seriously."

"It's no problem," I said. "It's what family is for. Love you, man."

"Love you too."

Jack

I CLOSED MY LAPTOP AND LEANED BACK IN MY OFFICE CHAIR, rubbing at my temples. I'd found it impossible to concentrate. Not because Connor was in my house, but because I hadn't slept well last night.

You didn't sleep well because you kept picturing Connor's gorgeous body lying in bed with you. Maybe your dick sandwiched between those tight ass cheeks of his while you stroked his cock, and he begged you to let him cum.

I pushed back my chair and stood, ignoring my urge to find an excuse to walk down the hallway to the library and "check" on the progress of the bookshelves. Not that I had to hide away in my office while he worked, but it was better... safer if I didn't see him. Connor didn't even realize I was home. When I came home from the office, his truck wasn't in the driveway.

I assumed he'd finished early for the day, but about an hour ago, I'd heard the front door slam and the heavy tread of his footsteps as he walked past my office to the library. I'd spent the last week and a half avoiding him as best as I could, and it was ridiculous how out of sorts I felt about it. I barely knew the guy. Not seeing him every day shouldn't be the problem it was.

Feeling restless, I walked to the window and stared out into the backyard.

"Holy fuck," I muttered.

Connor was in the backyard. He'd set up his table saw in the flat grassy area of the yard about ten feet from the pool, and he was currently measuring a plank of wood. It was a hot day, and he'd stripped off the "Hayes Carpentry" work shirt he usually wore. I stared at his upper body in the white tank top. I was in good shape and worked out regularly, but Connor's upper body was jacked with muscle and beyond sexy.

I could barely stop myself from unzipping my pants and yanking on my dick as I watched Connor bend down and pick up a piece of wood, his jeans clinging to his ass.

"Fuck," I said, "what I wouldn't give to tap that ass."

"You shouldn't swear in front of little kids."

The voice coming from behind me made me scream and clutch at the windowsill before I whipped around. I stared at the tiny human standing in the doorway of my office. She looked to be about five or six, and her blonde hair was pulled away from her face in two pigtails. She wore a pink t-shirt and green shorts, and sandals that lit up as she walked toward me.

"When my daddy swears in front of me, he has to put a

dollar in my piggy bank." The little girl stopped in front of me, staring expectantly at me.

"Who are you?" I said.

"I'm Eva. Who are you?"

"Jack," I said. "How did you get in my house, Eva?"

"Uncle Connor had a key," she said. "Do you have any cookies? I'm hungry."

"I don't have any cookies," I said.

Her face dropped, and feeling weirdly guilty, I said, "Cookies are bad for you."

She shrugged. "Only if you eat a lot of them."

She walked over to my desk and ran her hand across the top of it. "I like your desk. It's shiny."

"Thank you."

"I like your whole house," she said. She glanced at the open doorway. "Uncle Connor said I had to stay in the library because I'm not supposed to be here, but I got bored, and I had to pee."

"Did you find the bathroom?" I asked.

"Yes. Your tub is huge. I could go swimming in it." She moved to the bookshelf behind my desk and stared up at the books. "You have a lot of books."

"I like reading," I said.

"Me too. Have you read any Beverly Cleary books?"

"No," I said.

She frowned. "They're really good books. I'll bring you one of mine so you can read it. I'm only in kindergarten, but my teacher said I read at a second-grade level. Auntie Angie says it's because I'm really smart."

She joined me at the window, staring up at me. "I heard Uncle Connor telling Daddy that you're rich. How much money do you have?"

"A lot," I said.

"I have thirty dollars in my piggybank." She grinned at me. "Uncle Connor swears a lot when he's watching football. Auntie Nora says he's gonna pay for my college education all by himself. But I'm gonna use the money to buy myself a Barbie car. Did you know it drives just like a real car? It has a gas pedal and a brake and everything. Avril in my class got a Barbie car for her birthday. She let some of the kids drive it at her birthday party, but she said I couldn't. She said I would drive it too fast and crash it."

"Would you?" I said.

She thought for a minute before nodding. "Yeah, proba-bly. Uncle Shepherd says you have a lot of cars. My favourite car is the Ford Mustang Shelby GT500. What's yours?"

"Mine is -"

"Eva!" Connor came rushing into the office. There was sawdust clinging to his face, and he was wearing his work shirt again.

"Eva, I told you to stay in the library while I was outside." Connor scooped her up in his arms.

"I had to pee," Eva said.

He gave me an apologetic look. "Sorry, Eva's dad had a work emergency, and I was the only one who could pick her up from school. He'll be here in, like, five minutes to pick her up."

"Jack has a huge tub," Eva informed him. "I could go swimming in it." She gave me a smile meant to charm. "If I brought my bathing suit, could I go swimming in your tub?"

"Eva, you're not -"

"I have an actual pool you can swim in," I said.

Her eyes widened. "You have a pool?"

"I do."

Eva squealed with excitement before wrapping her little arms around Connor's thick neck. "Uncle Connor, can I come here tomorrow after school and go swimming in Jack's pool?"

"No, honey. I'll be working while I'm here, and you can't go swimming by yourself."

Eva sighed. "But I've never swum in a real pool before, just the stupid lake."

"You're welcome to come by on Saturday and take her swimming," I said.

Connor blinked at me. "Oh, uh…"

"Yay!' Eva shouted. "I'm gonna wear my purple bathing suit and bring Mr. Perkins so he can go swimming too!"

"Are you sure about this?" Connor said to me.

Eva cut him a look. "Uncle Connor, don't ruin this for me."

I burst out laughing, and even Connor grinned as Eva clapped her hands. "I'm gonna swim in a pool!"

Connor's phone buzzed, and he pulled it out of his pocket. "Your dad is here to pick you up, honey."

"Okay. I'll see you on Saturday, Jack," Eva said, her little face beaming with happiness.

"Hold on," I said and pulled my wallet out of my pocket as I joined Connor and Eva. I took out a dollar bill and held it out to Eva.

She took it from me and said, "You owe me two dollars."

A puzzled look on his face, Connor said, "What's this about?"

"Jack swore in front of me," she said.

"Only once," I said.

"Nu-uh, you said two bad words." Eva slung her free arm around Connor's neck, the dollar bill I'd given her held tightly in the other hand. "Jack was looking out the window, and he said, 'fuck, what I wouldn't give to tap that ass.' Ass is a swear word too."

My face turned the colour of crimson, and so did Connor's. Eva stared at both of us. "Why are your faces so red? You look funny."

I didn't – couldn't – reply as Eva said, "Ass is a swear word, right, Uncle Connor?"

"Yeah, Eva." Connor was looking everywhere but at me.

My face on fire, I snagged another dollar bill from my wallet and held it out wordlessly to Eva.

"Thank you, Jack," she said as she took it from me. "It was a pleasure doing business with you today."

Connor made a weird and muffled choking sound before spinning around and striding toward the door. "I'll take Eva to her dad and then get back to work."

CHAPTER 5

Connor

I was just cleaning up for the day when Jack stepped into the library. I hadn't seen him today, even though I knew he was at the house. I wasn't surprised. After what happened with Eva yesterday, I was pretty sure I would build his entire library without ever seeing Jack's face again.

I had thought about texting him, a casual *hey, sorry for bringing my niece to work with me, and don't worry about her overhearing that you want to fuck me*, but how exactly did one word that casually?

"Hey," I said as I finished sweeping up the last of the sawdust and dumped it into a pail. "How's it going?"

"Good." Jack wore a t-shirt and a pair of shorts that revealed muscular thighs and calves. The man obviously did not skip out on leg day, and I, for one, appreciated his dedication.

I glanced at his face. He hadn't shaved, his eyes were bloodshot, and he looked tired and a little out of sorts.

He scratched at the stubble on his face and said, "I need to apologize for yesterday."

"It's no big deal."

"It is a big deal," he said with a frown. "It's a very big deal, and I need you to know that even though I thought I was alone, I still should not have said what I said, and I'm sorry."

"Okay. Thank you for the apology." It felt weird to accept an apology for something that hadn't bothered me in the least, but the man looked rough and much more upset about it than the situation called for. Maybe if I kept it low-key and just accepted his apology, it would stop him from freaking the fuck out more than he already was.

He took a deep breath, one hand coming up to run through his dark hair. His motion made it stick up in an *I just rolled out of bed* look. It would have been sexy as hell if I wasn't worried my newest client was about to have a nervous breakdown because I knew he wanted to fuck me.

He turned to leave, then turned back around, staring at me earnestly. "Look, I get that there's this whole *a gay man will try to turn every straight man he sees* bullshit idea among the straights, and I want to be clear that despite what happened yesterday, it isn't true. I'm embarrassed that as a gay man, my actions yesterday reinforced that idea, and I want to be clear that I do not prey on straight men, and I won't ever do or say anything to make you uncomfortable again. You have my word on that."

"Jack, I'm gay," I said.

"You're not," he said with a look of shock that was almost comical.

"Pretty sure I am," I said.

"But my gaydar is…"

"Your gaydar?" I laughed. "I haven't heard that term since I was a teenager."

He flushed and stared silently at me for a moment. "You're gay."

"Card carrying member," I said. "Don't make me show you my browser history to prove it, though. I don't think our relationship is at the kink sharing point quite yet."

Stop flirting, asshole.

He looked away, scrubbed his hand through his hair again, and then said, "Aw, fuck. I'm an asshole *and* an idiot."

"Don't worry about it," I said.

He blew his breath out before glancing at his watch. "My workday is officially over, and it looks like yours is too. Can I offer you a beer?"

At my hesitation, he said quickly, "A friendship beer."

A grin crossed my face. "I'd love a friendship beer."

"When did you come out?" I took a drink of beer as Jack grabbed his own from the minifridge.

He sat down at the table beside me and sipped at his beer. The outdoor kitchen setup he had was pretty sweet. Hell, it was nicer than the kitchen in my apartment, and I was certain the chair cushion my ass was sitting on cost more than my couch.

"I was seventeen when I told my dad, but he'd known for a while," Jack said. "He let me tell him when I was ready, though, and I appreciated it. I figured it out when I hit puberty and realized it was watching the grade twelve guys' volleyball team and not the girls' team that gave me unexpected erections."

I laughed and tipped my beer to him. "Basketball team for me."

We clinked beer bottles and drank. "What about your mom? Was she cool with it?"

"She died when I was twelve," Jack said.

"I'm sorry," I said.

He stared pensively at the pool. "I don't know what I would have done without my dad. He was a rock after Mom died, even though I knew he was devastated and lost without her. My teenage years would have been horrible if it hadn't been for his support."

"You're still close with him?"

A flicker of pain crossed his face. "He died four years ago from pancreatic cancer."

"I'm sorry," I said again. "My dad died when I was fifteen, so I understand the grief."

He studied me. "I'm sorry to hear that. You're close with your brother, right?"

"He's one of my best friends," I said. "But honestly, I'm close with all of my family. There are six of us kids, and we all get along really well for the most part. We have our moments, but we've always got each other's backs. It's why I brought Eva with me yesterday. James needed my help. But I promise I won't make a habit of bringing my six-year-old niece to the job site. It was an emergency yesterday."

"It's fine," he said. "I enjoyed meeting her."

I laughed. "Yeah, she's a great kid. Super fucking smart. My sister Angie is after James to have her IQ tested because she thinks she might be at a genius level, but James isn't interested. He wants Eva just to be a kid and enjoy her life without being labeled."

"I haven't been around a lot of kids," Jack said, "but her vocabulary seemed crazy good for her age."

"It is," I said proudly. "She reads a lot and at a grade two level. She's so damn smart. She's gonna change the world."

We sat in silence for a minute before I said, "Do you have siblings?"

He shook his head. "No, it was just my dad and me. Our house was often very... quiet."

I smiled a little. "My childhood was utter chaos. We lived in a three-bedroom rowhouse with my Mom and my Nan, and there wasn't much privacy or space. It's why I love your house so much... there's plenty of space."

He smiled. "My interior designer feels like I took the minimalist look a little too far, but I like the clean lines and neatness of it. Other than books and cars, personal stuff isn't all that important to me."

"How long have you been collecting books?"

"Since I was a kid. My grandfather loved books as well. I have a few from his collection that are special to me. I think my grandfather's love of books is partially what inspired my father to start a publishing company."

"Did you want to work with your father, or was it an expected thing?" I asked.

"I wanted to work with him. After I got my business degree, I joined the company officially. It was struggling at the time. Dad only had a few authors, and none of them were big names. Over the next few years, we turned it around, and now we're the most successful independent small-scale publishing company in the country."

"Small scale?" I said. "You have more than a few successful and well-known authors as your clients."

He grinned at me. "I didn't know you were that into the publishing world, Connor."

A shiver went down my back, and my dick twitched at the sound of my name on his lips. "I did some research on the company before I met with you."

"So, tell me more about your furniture making business," Jack said.

"It's not much of a business at the moment, more of a hobby," I said. "But I'm hoping to turn it into something more in the future. Once I've turned my current company into a carpentry powerhouse and have handed the reins to a trusted employee, of course."

"Of course," Jack said with a laugh. "Well, I'm very impressed with what you've done so far in the library. The wall of bookshelves you've completed looks amazing, and I'm impressed at how much you've finished already. My experience with contractors hasn't always been this positive when it pertains to how quickly they finish a job."

"I pride myself on being efficient," I said. Jack didn't need to know that he was currently my only client, which made it a hell of a lot easier to focus my attention solely on his library.

He took another drink of beer. "Well, I'm definitely happy with the work. Judy and William down the street have been talking about tearing down their old pool house and rebuilding a new one for the last six months. If you'd like, I could give them your contact information."

"Yes, please do." I tried to hide the excitement on my face and in my voice, but it was tough.

"Great. I'll pass on your number."

We drank in silence for a few minutes. I was surprised at how much I liked Jack. Sure, I'd been lusting after him since I met him, but I hadn't expected to like him. He wasn't what I thought, not arrogant or demeaning at all, and it had been kind of him to invite Eva to swim in the pool tomorrow.

"So, are you sure you're good with Eva coming by tomorrow to swim?" I asked.

"Yes. I have a meeting in the morning, but anytime after one works," he said.

When I didn't reply, he said, "It isn't a problem, Connor."

"Thank God," I said, "because it's all she's talked about since you mentioned it."

Jack laughed. "I'm glad she's excited."

"Excited is not the word. More like... bouncing off the walls. Poor James practically had to wrestle her into bed last night."

Jack's phone buzzed, and he glanced at the screen before texting rapidly. I finished the last of my beer and stared at the pool. I was meeting Shepherd and Tristan for dinner at seven-thirty, and it was almost seven. With something like regret in my stomach, I smiled at Jack when he set his phone down. "I should get going."

"You don't have to go," he said. "Sorry about that. I just needed to reassure an author freaking out over a bad review. Anyway, I'm grilling steaks and veggie kabobs if you wanted to stay for dinner."

"Thanks, but I'm meeting Shepherd and Tristan for dinner."

"Right, of course, it's Friday night. You would have plans." Jack cleared his throat. "I forget that not everyone's a workaholic like me."

For a moment, I was tempted to ask him if he wanted to come with me. And not because it would be nice not to feel like the third wheel at dinner, but because I wanted to know more about him. Wanted to sit in a small booth with our shoulders and our thighs brushing and pretend that Jack was my...

Your what? Your boyfriend? Grow the fuck up, Connor. A great ass and a good personality don't mean shit, and you know it. Christ, has it been that long since you got laid that you imagine a relationship with the first guy who shows inter-est? You and Jack are complete opposites.

"Connor? You okay?" Jack stared at me from across the table.

I stood. "Yeah, I'm good. Thanks for the beer. I'll see you tomorrow around one-thirty?"

"Sure. See you then." Jack stood, and I waved him off.

"I'll let myself out. Good night, Jack."

"Good night, Connor."

CHAPTER 6

Jack

"Hi, Jack! I'm here to go swimming! I brought you one of my Beverly Cleary books. This is my Auntie Nora. She wanted to go swimming too, and Uncle Connor said she couldn't. But then Auntie Nora threatened to tell Nan about the time Uncle Connor kissed Toby Peterson in the vestibule at church when he was ten, and Uncle Connor folded like a card table."

I burst into laughter as the curvy woman with pink hair, tattoos, and a septum ring grinned at me, and Connor turned a shade of red I didn't think was possible.

Eva skipped into the house past me, wearing a purple polka-dot bathing suit and carrying a book bag in one hand and a purple plastic blob with eyes in the other. "Doesn't Jack have a nice house, Auntie Nora? It's so pretty."

"Hi." The young woman shifted the giant beach bag she carried to her other hand and stuck her hand out. "I'm Connor's sister, Nora."

"Hi, Nora, I'm Jack." I shook her hand.

Connor, his face still red, said, "If Nora staying to swim is a problem, she'll leave."

"And risk Nan finding out about you kissing Toby Peterson?" I said. "Not a chance. I don't want my library going unfinished because your grandma has grounded you."

Nora laughed. "Oh, I like you."

"Come in," I said.

Nora and Connor stepped inside, and as Connor shut the door, I tried not to be completely obvious about checking him out. He was wearing a t-shirt and a pair of swim trunks, and his thighs were making my mouth water. They bulged with muscle, like every other part of his body. Picturing those beautiful thighs spread wide in my bed while I slid my dick deep inside of him made me very glad I hadn't changed into my swim trunks yet.

"Eva, don't touch!" Connor hurried over to where Eva had her hands pressed flat against the patio door leading out to the backyard. "You're leaving prints, honey."

"It's fine," I called as Nora looked me up and down.

"You're a tall drink of water, aren't you?" she said. "I can see why Tristan said you were hot. Hey, you don't happen to play for both teams, do you?"

"Sorry," I said. "I'm only into dudes."

She sighed. "Story of my life. Seriously though, if it's a problem that I'm here too, I can -"

"It isn't," I said. "I'm happy to have you guys over for a swim whenever you want."

"Ooh, you're gonna regret saying that," she said with another laugh. "But isn't that just like a Libra? Nothing makes you happier than seeing everyone living their best life."

"How did you know I was a Libra?" I asked.

She shrugged. "I'm good at stuff like that. Connor's a Leo like me."

"Okay," I said slowly, not sure what she was getting at.

She smiled. "A Leo and a Libra make an excellent match."

I could hear Connor's sigh from across the room. "Nora, you promised."

"I promised not to be weird or do any edibles before coming over," Nora said.

"You're being weird," Connor said.

"She's not being weird," I said.

Nora hooked her arm around mine and said in a low voice, "But I am the teensiest bit high. Don't tell Connor."

I laughed and made a zipping motion across my lips. Nora squeezed my arm. "You and I are going to get along marvellously, Jack. I can feel it in my bones."

"UNCLE CONNOR, LOOK AT ME! LOOK AT ME! I'M SWIMMING!" Eva's shrieks of delight echoed across my backyard.

"Great job, sweetheart," Connor said.

Eva, her small body held up by water wings on both arms, doggie paddled around the shallow end of the pool under the watchful eye of Nora.

"Jack, can you please take Mr. Perkins. He's tired of swimming," Eva said.

"Sure." I stood up from the lounger and walked over to the pool, bending over to take the purple plastic blob with eyes from Eva.

"Thank you, Jack," Eva said.

"You're welcome." I straightened and turned around, not

failing to miss the way Connor, stretched out on the lounger next to mine, looked away quickly. I'd bet Mr. Perkin's blobby plastic life that he'd been checking out my ass.

Trying not to strut, I returned to my chair, setting Mr. Perkins on the empty one beside me before stretching my legs out. "You didn't swim for very long."

Connor laughed. "I like swimming, but I also enjoy lying in the sun like a lizard."

I took a drink of lemonade. "Even though I know it's bad for me, I also enjoy soaking up some sun."

"We're wearing sunscreen," Connor said with a grin. "Speaking of which…I'm due for another coat." He sat up and rummaged through Nora's beach bag for the bottle of sunscreen.

I tried not to drool as he smoothed it over his legs, arms, chest, and abdomen. While I was proud of my six pack, it was a dog's breakfast compared to Connor's eight pack.

I tore my gaze from Connor's perfect body before I embarrassed myself with a full-blown erection. I hated my lack of control around him. I wasn't used to lusting after someone I barely knew, but seeing Connor in nothing but swim trunks had me hanging on to my sanity by my finger-nails. Sleeping with the guy I hired to work for me was a colossal mistake. I knew that. So, why couldn't I think of anything but fucking him?

"Nora, come do my back!" Connor hollered.

She shook her head. "Nope. Busy."

"You're not busy," Connor said.

"Sure I am." She had boosted herself and Eva up onto the floating pool lounge and they were both stretched out on it as it floated around the pool.

"You're not," Connor said.

"I am. Ask Jack to help," she said with a sweet smile at both of us.

Connor muttered something that almost sounded like a death threat as Nora blew him a kiss and then used her hand to paddle the lounge float around, so their backs were to us.

Connor went to stick the sunscreen back into the bag, and I sat up and swung my legs over the side of the lounger. "It's fine. Give me the sunscreen."

"I'll keep lying on my back," he said. "It's no big deal."

"You never roast a chicken on only one side," I said solemnly.

Connor laughed. "Did you just compare me to a chicken?"

I grinned at him, and he relented and handed over the sunscreen, then turned on his lounger to face the other way. I inched a little closer as Connor said, "Apparently, I need to up my weights during my workouts if I remind you of a chicken."

I squirted some sunscreen onto my hands, already drooling at the thought of getting my hands on Connor's gorgeous back. I was such a fucking pervert. "A really muscular chicken."

He laughed. "Thanks, that makes it so much…"

His voice died in his throat the moment my hands touched his back. His skin was warm and smooth, and I wanted to lick a path from the bottom of his spine to the top. Instead, I rubbed the sunscreen into his skin, trying to keep my hands steady and my dick from ripping a hole right through my swim trunks.

Fuck, this was a bad idea.

Connor's body had tensed the moment I touched him. Like I was on autopilot, I moved my hands to his shoulders and rubbed and kneaded. He groaned, his head dropping forward.

"Feel good?" My voice was low, and I could hear the lust in it.

"Really good," Connor muttered.

My hands slick with sunscreen, I massaged his upper shoulders and neck as Connor made soft groans and moans that made me wish Eva and Nora weren't with us. I glanced over at the pool. The float was still turned around, and I could hear Eva chattering away to Nora, but they couldn't see us.

Madness screaming through my veins, I leaned forward until my chest was nearly touching Connor's back. I moved my hands to his lower back and rubbed firmly. Connor moaned, and his head fell back, landing on my shoulder with a soft thunk.

Still rubbing his back, I leaned even closer until Connor's upper back pressed against my chest. I stared over his shoulder at the way his swim trunks were tented. Now my mouth did start to water, and I slid my hands around his trim waist to his flat stomach. When I rubbed his abdomen, Connor made another low moan.

"Fuck, that feels good."

"I like making you feel good, Connor," I breathed into his ear. "I like the way you moan when I touch you."

His hands clenched down on his knees when I used one finger to trace just above the waistband of his trunks. The fabric strained at the crotch. I could see the outline of the head of his dick against the thin material, and my control snapped.

I needed to touch Connor's dick. Needed to feel how fucking amazingly thick it would be and how velvety soft the skin was. My cock a raging hot stone against Connor's back, I started to slide my hand inside Connor's trunks.

He made a grunt of surprise and grabbed my hand, pushing it away as he sat up and stared over at the pool. "Not in front of Eva."

"Fuck," I said. "I'm sorry, I shouldn't have -"

Connor stood and walked into the house without another word. My stomach in knots and my cock going limp, I stared unseeingly at the grove of apple trees beyond the pool as the patio door slid shut.

Holy shit, what the fuck did I just do?

"Jack!" Eva hollered.

"Yeah?" My voice was a low croak.

"Would it be okay if I had some more lemonade?" Eva peered around the float, trailing one hand in the water. "I'm pretty thirsty."

"Of course," I said. "There's more in the house. I'll get it for you."

"I can get it," Nora said as she craned her head to stare at me. "You stay where you are and relax."

"It's fine." I stood up. "I don't mind."

I walked into the house. Connor was nowhere to be seen, and cursing myself in my head, I grabbed the jug of lemonade from the fridge. I grabbed a clean glass, but my fingers were still slick from the sunscreen, and the glass slipped out of my hand and shattered on the floor.

"Shit."

Happy I was wearing sandals to protect my feet, I bent and picked up a larger piece of glass and immediately cut my finger on the sharp edge.

"For fuck's sake!" I snarled.

"What's wrong?"

I straightened and turned, staring at Connor standing just behind me. "Don't come any closer. You're barefoot, and I dropped a glass."

He stared at the blood on my hand. "You're bleeding."

"Just a small cut." I stepped over the broken glass. "There are Band-Aids in the half bath." I pushed past him. My shame at what I'd almost done outside was still raging through me, and I couldn't meet Connor's gaze. "I'll be right back."

I walked to the bathroom and opened the medicine cabinet, searching for the Band-Aids as I kept my hand over the sink. Blood dripped from my finger, and I jerked all over when Connor said, "Let me look for them."

He stepped into the bathroom, closing the door and trapping me in the suddenly much-too-small room with him. I took a step back, my back hitting the wall as Connor joined me at the medicine cabinet. Despite my shame, just being this close to his big, tanned body was making me fucking hard again.

He found the Band-Aids, ripped one open, and crooked his finger at me. "Come here."

"It's fine," I said. "I think it's stopped bleeding now."

He stared at my finger. "You're getting blood on the floor. Come here, Jack."

I sighed and joined him at the sink, hoping like fuck he didn't see the bulge at my crotch as he rinsed my finger, dried it, and wrapped the Band-Aid around it.

"There," he said, then surprised me by pressing a gentle kiss against my finger. "All better."

I swallowed hard. "Connor, about what just happened. I shouldn't have -"

I was cut off with a muffled grunt when Connor pushed me back against the wall and kissed me hard. His tongue pushed against my lips, and I parted them, moaning when he thrust his tongue into my mouth.

His lips were firm and warm from the sun, and I could taste the sourness of the lemonade on his tongue. As Connor pressed his body against mine, I slid my hands into his hair and held tight before slanting my mouth over his and taking control of the kiss.

Connor's pelvis pushed against mine. My erection was back, and we both gasped when our cocks rubbed against each other. I explored Connor's back and chest with my hands, teasing his flat nipples and running my fingers up and down the bumps of his ribs.

He reached around and squeezed my ass, pushing up tight against me and making my cock weep with precum.

"Fuck," Connor muttered against my mouth, "I want to suck your dick so fucking much."

"Christ," I moaned, "don't say that, or I'll have you on your knees right here."

Connor stared at me, the look on his face one of hot lust. It took half a second for me to move my hands to his shoulders and push. "On your knees, Connor."

He dropped to his knees. It was a small bathroom, and his toes pushed against the far wall, but he reached eagerly for my swim trunks, pulling down the front of them and making a low sound of approval when my cock popped out.

I slapped my hand over my mouth, muffling my cry of pleasure when Connor immediately sucked me into his mouth. He cleaned away the precum that coated the tip of it, and the feel of his soft wet tongue made every nerve ending in my body blaze into life.

When he took me deep, his lips sliding down over my cock and his hand squeezing the base of it, I couldn't help myself. I clamped my hands on the back of his skull and fucked his mouth with hard and out-of-control thrusts. Connor stared up at me, his dark eyes never leaving mine, as I moaned and panted.

"So good, baby," I whispered as I slid my cock in and out

of his mouth. "You're so fucking good at this. Can you take more for me?"

Connor leaned closer, his nostrils flaring, and – oh holy fuck – I could barely stifle my shout of pleasure when he deep throated me. My back bowed, and my head fell back at the feel of his wet mouth surrounding my entire fucking dick. He pulled back and did it again, his throat working around my dick and his hands digging into my ass.

"Oh fuck!" My voice was too loud. "Oh fuck, baby. I'm gonna cum. I can't… I'm gonna cum… oh fuuuuck."

Connor didn't release me at my warning. Instead, he bobbed his head faster, his lips sucking hard on my dick, his tongue teasing the thick vein on the underside. I buried my face into the crook of my elbow, the other hand still clamped around Connor's head, shouting hoarsely as my orgasm washed over me and I blew my load down Connor's throat.

He swallowed all of it, keeping his lips wrapped tight around my dick until I was spent and shuddering. He cleaned the tip of my dick with his tongue, then pulled my swim trunks up and stood. I leaned against the wall, panting for breath and shuddering.

"Holy fuck," I whispered. "You deep throated me. I've never been deep throated before."

Connor grinned. "You're welcome."

"Holy fuck," I repeated. "I mean… holy fuck."

Connor's smile widened. "This is, hands down, the best reaction I've ever gotten to giving a blow job."

I blinked before reaching for him and pulling him in tight against me. His skin was still warm from the sun, and I gave him an almost chaste kiss before sliding my hand down his flat abdomen. "Your turn."

He hissed out a breath as I slid my hand into his shorts

and wrapped my fingers around his cock. "Fuck, you're thick."

He moaned in reply, his forehead resting against mine as I jacked him with long, slow strokes. I was about to get on my knees when there was a knock at the bathroom door. We both froze, staring at each other with wide, guilty eyes, when Eva said, "Jack? Are you in here? I came to get my lemonade, but there's glass all over the kitchen. Did you hurt yourself?"

"Just a small cut, Eva," I said as I slipped my hand out of Connor's shorts. "I'm okay."

"Okay. Do you know where my Uncle Connor is?"

"Uh, I'm not sure," I said with a guilty look at Connor.

He stared at his obvious erection before making a *do something* motion with his hand.

"I'm gonna get my lemonade, okay?" Eva said. "I'll be careful not to step in the glass."

"No," I said quickly before pushing Connor back, so he was hidden by the door when I opened it. "I'll help you, honey."

"Sure, okay. Thank you, Jack." Eva smiled up at me as I closed the bathroom door, and we walked toward the kitchen. "I'm having a lot of fun today, and so is Mr. Perkins. I hope I can come back and swim again."

I took one final look at the bathroom before smiling down at her. "Of course, you can come back and swim again."

"And Mr. Perkins too?"

"Yes," I said. "Mr. Perkins too."

CHAPTER 7

Connor

"You did what?" I paced back and forth in Shepherd's small backyard, glaring daggers at Nora with every step.

Unfazed by my anger, she repeated, "I invited him to family dinner tomorrow night, and he said yes."

"Are you insane?" I asked.

"Of course not. Mom had me tested, remember?"

Tristan snorted laughter, and Shepherd grinned at him. "She's not kidding."

"Why?" I said. "Why would you do that, Nora?"

"Because Mom wanted to say thanks for letting Eva swim in his pool last weekend, and because he's funny and good looking, and because the sexual tension between the two of you is off the charts. I'm doing you a favour, big brother."

"No," I snapped. "You are not doing me a fucking favour, Nora. You're just butting in where you don't belong, like you always do."

"Connor," Shepherd said.

The smile dropped from Nora's face. Her eyes watering and her face red, she stood up and walked into Shepherd's house without another word.

"Way to go, dickhead," Shepherd said. "What the fuck is up with you today?"

I glanced at Tristan. He stood from his lawn chair and said, "I'm going to check on Nora."

I shot him a grateful look as he headed into the house. I sank into his empty chair and said, "Last Saturday, I gave Jack a blow job in his half bathroom."

When Shepherd didn't say anything, I looked over at him. "Aren't you going to say something?"

"What do you want me to say?" he said.

"That I'm an idiot, and I made a terrible mistake. That I'm lucky I haven't gotten fired for sucking my client's dick."

"I could say all of that if it makes you feel better," Shepherd said. "But considering I'm sleeping with my employee, I don't think I'm the right person to chastise you for sucking your client's dick. Besides, how would saying any of that help the situation with Jack?"

"There's no situation with Jack," I said. "I haven't even seen him since Saturday. He's been at the office all week. He's gone when I get there and doesn't return until I'm gone. I stayed until eight on Thursday night, and he never showed. He's avoiding me."

"So, there's a situation with Jack," Shepherd said.

"Fuck," I muttered. "What was I thinking? I wasn't thinking, that's the problem. This is all your fault, Shepherd."

"How is it my fucking fault?" Shepherd said.

I stood and paced again. "You could have mentioned how fucking hot and sexy Jack was."

"I don't think he's hot or sexy," Shepherd said. "Don't blame me for your dick not behaving."

"I shouldn't have done it, I know I shouldn't have, but we had this moment and... Jack isn't at all who I thought he would be. You know? He's funny and not arrogant, and he bought some of my custom furniture for fuck's sake!"

"He's a good guy," Shepherd agreed.

"He is, but that doesn't mean I want him meeting the entire family or seeing the home where I grew up. He was an only child, and you know it's gonna be too much for him. He's not used to the... chaos."

"Tristan was an only child, and he fits right in," Shepherd said. "Maybe Jack will too."

"Tristan doesn't have more money than God," I said. "Jack's house is... it's so different from Ma's house or my apartment or... he's a millionaire, for God's sake."

"If you're gonna have a relationship with the guy, you have to stop being ashamed of who you are and where you come from," Shepherd said.

I glared at him. "Fuck off, Shepherd. I'm not ashamed of who I am or of my family."

"But you're worried that if you start dating Jack, he'll look down on you eventually, just like Darryl did," Shepherd said.

"I'm not interested in dating him," I said. "At all."

"You sure? Because you're freaking out a whole lot about Jack seeing our family home for a guy you're not interested in."

"I just think there needs to be a line drawn. Jack is my client and your customer– I need to keep things professional between us, and professional doesn't include having him over for dinner at my mom's house," I said.

Shepherd laughed. "Professional line? Buddy, you dove over that line the moment you sucked his dick."

"It was a mistake," I said.

"Do you really think that?"

"It doesn't even matter what I think because I know for a fact that Jack does. Why else would he be avoiding me all week?"

"Why would he agree to come to dinner if he was trying to avoid you?" Shepherd said.

"He's being polite."

"Sure, that's it," Shepherd said.

We sat in silence for a few minutes, listening to the crickets sing and slapping at the occasional mosquito.

"Thanks for not judging me," I said.

Shepherd clapped me on the shoulder. "You know I'll always support you, man. I've always got your back."

"I know."

"Good." Shepherd took a drink of beer. "Now go apologize to Nora before I beat your ass for upsetting her."

Jack

"DADDY, JACK LIKED MY ROOM. HE SAID IT'S THE BEST room he's ever seen!" Holding my hand, Eva tugged me back into the small living room. Arrow immediately jumped up on me, barking excitedly and smacking at my thigh with his front paws.

"Arrow, no. Down, boy." Connor hurried over and pulled the friendly Pitbull away. "Sorry, Jack."

"It's fine. I don't mind."

Connor gave me a half-smile, half grimace that did nothing to hide the unease in his eyes. He'd been like this from the moment I stepped into his family home, apologizing over every little thing, barely looking me in the eye, and being much quieter than I was used to.

Of course, maybe he was the quiet one in his family. I grinned down at Eva as she tugged me over to where James was sitting on the couch with their youngest brother, Davey. They were watching football, and James gave Eva a distracted smile when she poked him in the thigh.

"Daddy! Pay attention to me."

"Sorry, Bunnykins. What's up?"

"Jack liked my room."

"That's great." James picked Eva up and dangled her upside down between his legs. "Hey, why don't you let Jack visit with Uncle Connor and Nan for a while. You're hogging him all to yourself."

"No, I'm not."

"Yes, you are," James said with a grin before tickling her belly. "It's not all about you, little Bunnykins."

"It should be," Eva said.

I laughed as Connor's mother, Alison, joined us. "Jack, sit with Nan and relax. Are you sure I can't get you another piece of pie? There's plenty."

"I'm sure." I patted my lean stomach. "Dinner was delicious, Mrs. Hayes. Thank you again."

"Call me, Alison," she said. "Can I get you a cup of coffee?"

"Ma," Connor was hovering just behind his mother, "Jack has a cappuccino machine at home. He doesn't drink instant coffee."

"I'd love a cup of coffee, Alison," I said. "Thank you."

"We have some of those fancy coffee creamers," Connor's grandmother said from her spot on the loveseat. "We have hazelnut and French vanilla. You should try a little in your coffee."

Connor made that weird face again. I smiled and said, "Sure. I'll try the hazelnut, please."

"Coming right up," Alison said.

Connor stepped closer as his mother retreated to the kitchen. His scent filled my nose, and I had to work hard not to lean down and kiss him.

"Look, you don't have to stay any longer if you don't want to," Connor said in a low voice.

"I want to stay," I said. "But if you want me to go…"

Surprise crossed Connor's face. "No, I… that is… I don't want you to feel obligated."

"I don't," I said.

"Okay, well, um…"

"Jack, seriously, what's your skin routine?" Connor's sister, Angie, joined us and studied my face. "Your skin glows."

"Angie," Connor said.

"What? I can't ask a guy what his skin routine is?"

"Not when you're making assumptions based on…"

"That he's gay?" Angie said. "It has nothing to do with that, and you know it. Not all gay men have skin routines. You and Shepherd are super gay, and you both have horrifyingly dull skin."

I laughed, and Angie grinned at me. "Spill it, Jack. What do you use?"

"It's actually a combination of products," I said.

"Ooh, hold on, I'm gonna make some notes on my phone," Angie said.

As I shared my skin routine with Angie, I watched Connor from the corner of my eye. He was leaning against the island, his gaze switching anxiously from me to his family and back to me. I'd known it would be awkward after what happened last Saturday, but I hadn't realized how awkward.

I'd been weirdly excited to get Nora's dinner invitation – the idea of meeting the rest of Connor's family was very appealing. Still, I hated how uncomfortable it seemed to make Connor. But the last time I'd seen him, he'd had my dick in his mouth, so maybe it was less about being uncomfortable and more about profound regret.

I cursed inwardly again that the insanity that was currently my work life meant I hadn't had a single chance to speak with him this week. While I knew it was wrong, I couldn't stop fantasizing the entire week about having Connor in my bed. It couldn't be anything more than that – dating wasn't an option. But was it so wrong for the two of us to explore this attraction between us for a night?

"Here's your coffee, Jack." Alison brought over a mug and handed it to me. "Go sit with Nan for a while."

"Sure." I smiled at Angie, who was typing the last of my skin recommendations into her phone. "Let me know if you have any more questions."

"Will do, thanks, Jack."

I took my coffee and eased onto the love seat next to Connor's grandmother. She had a blanket covering her lap despite the hot weather, and she patted my thigh gently. "How are you holding up, dearest? Nora said you were an only child, so all of this energy in the room must feel a little bonkers to you."

"Actually, I kind of love it," I said. "It's different, but my house was always so quiet growing up. I like this…"

"Chaos?" she said with a grin.

Nora crouched in front of her, placing her hands on her knees and smiling at her. "Nan, can I get you anything? Is your back still hurting?"

"No, sweetheart, the gummy you gave me has kicked in."

I almost choked on my sip of coffee, and Nora laughed.

"Do not tell Shepherd that I gave Nan an edible, Jack. He'll straight up murder me."

"He's against edibles?" I studied the tattooed mechanic. He was standing over by the island with Tristan and James, deep in conversation.

"No, he's against edibles for Nan," Nora said. "He's against anything that he thinks might be dangerous for her."

"Oh, please," Nan said. "I've been smoking weed for longer than that kid's been alive."

Nora giggled before standing and kissing Nan's cheek. "Just let me know if you need anything, Nan. Love you."

"Love you too, sweet girl." Nan watched Nora leave before turning back to me. "Don't I have just the best grand-children, Jack?"

"You do," I said. "Everyone in the family is wonderful."

"They really are," Nan said. "Especially Connor. Isn't he just brilliant? And so good with his hands. Do you know he builds custom furniture?"

"I do," I said. "I bought a coffee table from him, and I'm thinking of purchasing some nightstands."

"Isn't that marvelous," she said happily. "He's very good at carpentry, and he's working so hard to build his business, but I know his passion is in the furniture he creates. Unfortunately, he's in an apartment, and our back yard is too small here at the house, so Connor uses Shepherd's garage or back-yard to build his furniture. But he took me to his storage unit once to show me all the pieces he created, and I was gobs-macked by how good they are. He has enormous talent, don't you think?"

"Yes," I said as I studied him across the room. He'd joined Shepherd and the others, but he still looked distracted and uncomfortable. "You must be very proud of him."

"We are," Nan said as she stared at Connor for a moment.

"Now," she smiled at me, "tell me everything there is to know about Jack Walker."

———

"I HAD A NICE TIME TONIGHT. YOUR FAMILY IS GREAT," I SAID to Connor.

He shoved his hands in his pockets, staring at my car as the setting sun cast beams of light across his dark hair. "Thanks for coming to dinner. It meant a lot to my mom to say thank you for what you did for Eva."

"It was just a swim in the pool," I said.

He shrugged. "Maybe to you, but for Eva, it was something really special."

We both fell silent. That awkwardness was still between us, and my idea of inviting Connor back to my place was dying a slow and painful death. "Well, I guess -"

"I'm sorry," he said abruptly. "I'm sorry about Saturday and what I did to you."

"I liked what you did," I said. "I wanted you to do what you did. I started it, remember?"

He rocked back and forth on his toes. "No, you put sunscreen on my back, and then I – I lost my mind."

"I tried to touch your dick in front of your sister and your niece. If anyone needs to apologize, it's me. But what happened in that bathroom was amazing."

"You regret it," Connor said.

"No, I don't."

"You've avoided me all week." He finally met my gaze. "You've been at the office every day. That's not a coincidence."

"Do you remember on Friday when I said I had to reassure an author about a bad review?"

He nodded, and I said, "On Sunday morning, that same author said something stupid on social media because they were still pissed about the review. It's gone viral, and now the company has serious damage control to do, and the author doesn't understand what they've done wrong. That's why I've been at the office all week. It's been an utter shit show of meetings and conversations on how to handle the whole mess."

Connor scrubbed his hand through his hair. "Shit. I'm sorry. I just assumed that you were upset about Saturday."

"I get it. I thought about texting you a few times last week, but it didn't feel right. I wanted to have an actual conversation with you. But I worked late every night and left early every morning."

"Is the situation better now?"

"Honestly, I don't know yet. It's quieted down a bit, but the author is difficult to begin with, and she's still refusing to apologize. We've managed to convince her to stay off social media for a while, so that's a start, but I'm not sure how it's going to play out."

"That's rough," Connor said.

"It's not great. Anyway, I want to be perfectly clear that I have no regrets about what happened on Saturday and, in fact," I threw caution straight to the wind, "I'm wondering if you'd like to come by the house tonight so we can finish what we started."

He stared at me, his dark eyes unreadable in the shadows cast across his face. "I work for you."

"I know, but I can keep what we do tonight separate from our work relationship if you can. There's obviously an attraction between us, but I'm not looking for anything serious with you. We can just have one fun night together, can't we?"

The look on Connor's face had me reaching for his hand. "Connor? What's wrong?"

"Nothing," he said. He stared at our clasped hands, but the look on his face didn't exactly scream excitement over my suggestion. In fact, he looked sick to his stomach.

"I've stepped over the line, and I apologize," I said. "I thought you would be interested in -"

"I am," he said. "I'm interested, Jack."

"Are you?" I studied him carefully. "Because you look like you're going to throw up. Or punch me in the face."

His smile was utterly forced. "I'm good. I'll meet you at your place in, say, half an hour?"

The pit of my stomach was telling me something was very wrong. "Connor, if you're not interested, please just say so. It's not going to affect your work contract with me."

"I know," he said. "I'm interested." He took a deep breath and gave me a more natural smile that somewhat eased my apprehension. "Half an hour, okay?"

"Sure, okay. I'll see you soon." I didn't believe that Connor would show, but I smiled at him and climbed into my car. If he didn't, he didn't. I could only hope that he meant what he said.

CHAPTER 8

Connor

I parked in Jack's driveway and stared at the house. The blinds were drawn, but I could see the light peeking out from around the edges. I took a deep breath, still a little torn about whether I would go in or not.

You drove all this way, idiot. Is now the time to chicken out?

Probably not, but I was still reeling from the fact that Jack even wanted me here. I was so confident he'd regretted Saturday, so certain that he wanted nothing to do with me. Why would he? We were from two different worlds.

He only wants a night with you. Remember? You're just a fun distraction for him.

My stomach clenched. I did know that, so why was it such a kick in the gut to hear Jack say it?

Because he's different from who you thought he was, and you want more?

Maybe, but that wasn't what Jack wanted. Which left me with a choice. I could text Jack, tell him I'd changed my mind, and keep it strictly professional between us from now on. Or I could accept that while I might have growing feelings for Jack, he didn't feel the same for me, and I could just enjoy tonight for what it was.

I sat for another minute or so before climbing out of my truck and heading toward the door. Now that I'd decided, I made a conscious effort to push aside any misgivings or hurt feelings that Jack didn't want me the same way I wanted him. Tonight would give me the chance to be with Jack, and that would be enough. It had to be.

I rang the doorbell, and it opened almost immediately like maybe Jack had been hovering next to the door, waiting for me to make my choice. I could see the apprehension on his face mixed with surprise and a bit of relief.

"Hi, Connor."

"Hey."

He cleared his throat. "Come in."

I stepped inside, slipping off my shoes as Jack closed the door behind me. He'd changed to a t-shirt and shorts. My mouth watered at the way the shirt clung to his chest.

"Do you want a beer?" Jack said.

I stepped closer, sliding my arms around his waist and then nuzzling his neck. "Nope. Let's go to your bedroom."

He cupped my face and made me look at him. "Are you sure, absolutely sure, that this is what you want?"

"I am," I said, then grinned at him. "Unless you're suddenly nervous about seeing all this," I pointed to my body, "completely naked. Which, hey, I get. My body is a temple of awesomeness."

He laughed, the last of his tension melting away. "Seeing you completely naked is all I've thought about for the last two weeks."

"Good," I said. "Then take me to your bedroom."

He took my hand, and I followed him past the kitchen and down the hallway to his bedroom. His room was the size of my entire apartment, with a gas fireplace along one wall, French doors leading out into the backyard, and a king-size bed. It had the same minimalist décor as the rest of the house.

"This is nice," I said.

"Thanks." Jack pulled me back against him. I could feel his cock pushing against my ass, and I released my breath in a moan when Jack slid his hands under my shirt and traced the muscles of my abdomen. "You're so fucking hot, Connor."

I ground my ass against his dick, and his groan sent shivers down my spine. He kissed down the column of my throat, nipping at the base of my neck before turning me around. We kissed hotly, our tongues teasing, our hands roaming each other's bodies. When I squeezed his ass, Jack moaned into my mouth and reached for my shirt.

He pulled it off my body and made an admiring sound in the back of his throat before leaning down and sucking on one flat nipple.

"Fuuuck," I breathed, my hand cupping the back of his skull as my cock went impossibly hard. "Straight to the good stuff, huh?"

He shook his head, his hands unbuttoning my jeans and pushing them and my briefs down my legs. "No, this is straight to the good stuff."

He was on his knees with his mouth wrapped around my dick before I could blink. I moaned his name, watching with lust and pure need as Jack sucked my cock. Fuck, he was good at this. I ran my fingers through his thick hair as Jack went to work on my dick. His tongue slid up and down my shaft, teasing me with long wet strokes, as he cupped my balls and played gently with them. His finger slipped past my sac to press on my taint, and I cried out as precum spurted from the head of my dick. Jack cleaned it away, and I tugged on his arm until he moved his hand away.

He looked up at me. "You don't like that?"

"I fucking love it," I said hoarsely. "A little too much. If you don't want me cumming immediately and ruining the evening, you need to stop doing that."

He grinned and licked my cock again. "Baby, you cumming is not going to ruin the evening." He sucked on just the head of my dick, running his tongue around the ridge until I was practically jamming my cock back into his mouth. The hot wet pressure drove me crazy, and I was seconds from cumming when Jack pulled away.

"Fuck!" I muttered.

He grinned again before kissing along my upper thighs as his hands massaged my ass. "I want to fuck you, Connor."

"I want that too," I moaned. I fisted my cock, rubbing hard as Jack rose gracefully to his feet.

He tugged my hand away and kissed the palm. "That's for me to do tonight. Come on."

He helped me kick off my jeans and briefs and then led me toward the bed. My legs were trembling, and my cock was throbbing, and I was a little alarmed at how quickly Jack had brought me to the edge. It'd been a while for me, sure, but I usually had more self-control than that.

Jack pulled back the covers. "Get on the bed, Connor."

I relaxed on the bed, watching as Jack stripped off his clothes and then opened the nightstand next to the bed. The drawer stuck, and he grinned at me. "Now you see why I'm interested in looking at your nightstands."

"Right," I said distractedly. I was fisting my cock again. I couldn't help it. Just seeing Jack's dick, standing straight out from the short patch of pubic hair with the gleam of precum on the tip, made me so fucking horny I could barely control myself.

Jack took out the lube and the condom, setting them on top of the nightstand. His disapproving look as he watched the way I rubbed my cock, just made me hotter for him.

"If you make yourself cum, I won't fuck you, Connor."

That was enough to make me drop my hand from my dick. "That's not playing fair."

"I know," he said with a cat-like grin. "But who said I played fair?"

He relaxed on the bed beside me, his hand trailing lazily up and down my chest. "Your body is incredible."

"So is yours." I leaned forward and kissed his chest before circling his left nipple with my tongue. He moaned and moved closer until our cocks brushed, and we both groaned. I reached down and gripped us both, sliding my hand up and down while I teased Jack's nipple.

"Connor," he panted as his head fell back and his hips pumped, "remember what I told you."

"Technically, I'm jacking you off," I said before sucking at his nipple. "So, it doesn't count."

He half-laughed, half-groaned as I pumped us harder and faster. "Clever…"

"I'm excellent at finding loopholes in rules," I said.

He reached down and tugged my hand away. I admired his willpower since mine had flown out the window the second I felt his hot mouth on my dick. We kissed again, and I pulled away with a gasp. "Jack, I need you to fuck me."

"Soon." He kissed my neck and then coated his finger with lube before sliding his hand around to my ass. He slipped his finger between my cheeks and circled my tight hole. "I've thought about what it would be like to fuck you for weeks, Connor."

"Then maybe you should do it," I gritted out as my whole body broke out in goosebumps. "I'm dying here, Jack."

He teased his way across my chest with his tongue, tasting and licking and driving me mad as his finger continued to circle and press lightly. "Is that right?"

"Yes."

"How long has it been?" he said.

"Does it matter?"

His finger slowed, and he stared at me. "I want to know how slow I need to be when I first take your ass."

Another shiver through my body. "I can take whatever you give me."

"I'm sure you can," he said. "But why are you avoiding my question?"

"Because it's been a stupidly long time, and it's embarrassing."

"How long?"

"Eleven months."

"That's not embarrassing," he said.

"It's not great. But, in my defense, I was concentrating on building my business and... oh, oh holy fuck..."

Jack had pressed again and breached the tight ring of muscle. His slick finger probed a little deeper, and I groaned and reached for my dick as pleasure speared through my body.

Jack shook his head. "Don't, Connor, or I'll stop."

"Jack, please," I said. "I need..."

"Control," he said as his finger slid in and out of my ass. "Use it."

I gripped his arm instead, panting and moaning softly as Jack explored my ass. When he changed angles slightly, and his finger brushed against my prostate, my low groan turned into a loud cry. My hips jutted forward, my cock brushing against Jack's abdomen. Precum smeared across his stomach, and Jack smiled with satisfaction before kissing me again.

"Fuck, please, Jack," I moaned into his mouth.

His finger rubbed against my prostate again, and I nearly came right then and there. "Fuck!"

Jack nuzzled my neck as he slipped his finger out of my ass. "Get on your hands and knees, Connor."

"Thank fucking Christ," I mumbled.

Jack chuckled, and I watched as he rolled the condom on before slicking it with lube. I flipped to my stomach and got eagerly onto my hands and knees, staring over my shoulder at Jack as he kneeled between my open legs.

The lube was cold on my ass, but Jack rubbed it in quickly, warming it up before sliding two fingers into my ass and stretching me lightly. "You're so fucking tight, baby," he said in a low voice. "I'll try to go slow, but if I hurt you, just let me know."

"Just do it," I said, my voice strangled with need. "Fuck, Jack, this isn't my first time. I can handle your dick."

He laughed and leaned over to kiss my lower back as he slipped his fingers out. "I know." He moved a little closer, and his hard hands gripped my ass cheeks. He spread them apart, and I pushed back eagerly when I felt the head of his dick against my hole.

We both gasped when his cock slipped past the tight ring of muscle. Jack's fingers gripped my ass hard, and he pushed in a little further. I moaned at the sweet burn as he stretched me and rocked my hips back and forth as he pushed again.

"Just a little more, baby," he said. "You good?"

"Yeah," I panted. "It's good. It's all... fuck... good."

Jack's pelvis pressed against my ass cheeks as he slid all the way home. I let my head drop down and relaxed the muscles that had automatically tensed. Jack remained still, one hand rubbing my lower back, the other gripping my hip lightly.

"Okay?" he said after a minute or so.

"Yeah," I said. "Better than okay." I made a few experimental thrusts, and Jack's groan of lust made my cock harder than ever.

I reached for it, and Jack pushed my hand away. "For me, remember?"

"I kind of hate you right now," I said as Jack made a few long slow thrusts that curled my toes.

"No, you fucking love what I'm doing to you," Jack said. His hands smoothed down my thighs, and then he pressed on my lower back until I lowered my upper body to the bed. His hands returned to my hips and gripped tightly as he moved harder and faster. I clutched the sheets in both hands to stop myself from rubbing my dick as Jack's movements turned rough.

"Fuck, Jack, please," I moaned.

I could have shouted hallelujah when he pulled me back up until I was braced on my hands again. He reached under me and took my cock in his hand, setting a firm and furious pace of stroking that immediately had me on the edge.

"Christ, I'm not going to last," I groaned, my hips pumping hard as Jack's pelvis slapped against my ass.

"That's the idea." The control in Jack's voice was gone. "Touch yourself, baby. Make yourself cum while I fuck you."

His hand dropped from my dick, and I immediately took over, rubbing with long, hard strokes as Jack took my ass in a rough and frantic rhythm. The pleasure was building in my spine and pelvis, and when the head of Jack's dick brushed against my prostate, I came like a fucking firehose, moaning Jack's name.

He pumped hard and fast into me. I could barely keep

myself upright as Jack drove in deep and his hands clamped down hard around my hips. He made a hoarse drawn-out cry of pleasure before his body shook violently, and he pumped in and out a few more times.

Shuddering with the aftermath of my climax, I immediately fell onto my side the minute Jack pulled out of me. He climbed off the bed and headed to the bathroom. I kept my eyes closed, jerking a little when I felt the warm wet cloth on my stomach.

"Sorry," Jack said as he wiped the cum from my abdomen.

"Thanks," I said.

"My pleasure." He dropped the cloth in the laundry hamper and climbed into bed behind me, wrapping his arm around my waist and dropping a kiss against the back of my shoulder. "You okay?"

"Yeah, you?"

"Fantastic. That was amazing, Connor."

"It was."

He kissed my shoulder again before resting his head on the pillow behind me. It was nice lying in Jack's bed, the warmth of his hard body tucked against mine, my body completely sated in a way I'd never felt before.

I should have closed my eyes and gone to sleep, should have let myself just relax and drift off, the way I could tell that Jack was. Instead, my brain refused to shut off. I stared at the far wall, at the piece of art hanging on it that probably cost more than my truck, as remorse seeped in.

What just happened was the best sex of my life, and it would never happen again. Jack had made it clear he only wanted one night. Why I thought that would be fine was beyond me.

Because you were horny and you wanted him and because

you like him, you moron. Only, where has that got you? Nothing but a lifetime of regret that you'll never get to touch Jack again, never hear him moan your name or use that hot mouth of his on your dick to drive you crazy.

I moved restlessly in the bed. Jack's arm tightened around me, and he muttered something that was a bit too garbled for me to understand. He was almost asleep, and I was suddenly and intensely jealous that he had no second thoughts or regrets. This was easy for him. A nice satisfying fuck with the hired help, a night of fun to take his mind off a shit week at work, and that was it. No pesky feelings to deal with, no wishing he could have more.

Feeling sorry for myself, I sat up and pulled away from Jack's grip. I swung my legs over the side of the bed as Jack sat up behind me. "Wha? Connor, what's wrong?"

Christ, he sounded adorable when he was only half awake. "Nothing's wrong. Go back to sleep. It's getting late, and I need to go."

"Stay the night," he said.

"Thanks, but I can't. I have a meeting with another client early tomorrow before I start work here," I lied.

"Oh, okay."

Jack didn't sound disappointed. I tried not to take it personally. He was clear about what this was from the start.

He yawned and threw back the covers. "I'll walk you out."

"No need," I said as I pulled up my jeans and buttoned them. "I have a key, remember?"

"Right. Okay. See you tomorrow." Jack was already burrowing back under the covers.

I pulled my shirt on and left the bedroom, telling myself I hadn't just made the worse fucking mistake of my life.

CHAPTER 9

Jack

I turned into the parking lot of the storage place and parked in the empty spot next to Connor's truck. He was sitting in the driver's seat, staring at his phone, and I studied his face for a minute or two.

For the last four days, Connor had said and done all the right things, but there was still a distance between us that I couldn't seem to breech. Of course, I'd spent all of this week at the office downtown again and had only seen Connor twice, but both times, it felt awkward.

Or maybe I was just reading into it. It was bound to be somewhat awkward once you'd slept with someone you had no intention of sleeping with again, right? To be fair, my usual one-night stands weren't with someone I would then see in my own damn house for the next two weeks straight.

So, why did you do it then? Why the fuck did you sleep with Connor?

Because I'd wanted him. Desperately. Still did, in fact. I spent every night lying in bed, staring at the spot where

Connor had been, before masturbating to the memory of his perfect, tight ass, his delicious tasting dick, and the low sound of his voice pleading for me to touch him.

My cock was hardening just thinking about it, and, not for the first time, I regretted my decision to ask Connor for only one night.

So, tell him you've changed your mind. Ask if he'll sleep with you again. There's no harm in asking, right?

Maybe not, but I knew the answer would be no. The way Connor didn't quite meet my gaze now, that 'don't touch me' vibe that practically emanated from him, made it perfectly clear that he'd been satisfied with just one night. And now, most likely, seriously regretted it.

I sighed and climbed out of my car when I heard Connor's truck door open. Plastering a smile on my face, I said, "Hey, thanks for meeting me here. I'm sure you would have preferred just to go straight home."

"It's not a problem," he said. "I appreciate your interest in my work." He looked me up and down. I'd come straight from the office and was still wearing a suit. The brief flare of hope that maybe Connor was still into me disappeared when he turned away and said, "Follow me."

We walked past the rows of storage units until we got to one near the end. Connor unlocked the padlock, pulled the rattling, squeaking garage door up, and flicked on the light.

"So, the nightstands are back here." I followed him into the garage, staring with frank admiration at the pieces of furniture we passed.

I stopped next to a smaller sized bookshelf, admiring the gleam of the wood and the intricate designs carved into the front edge. "Connor, this is gorgeous."

"Thanks." He backtracked and joined me. "It's one of my first pieces, so I've improved a lot since then."

"Shit, for one of your first pieces, this is even more incredible."

A pleased look came over his face, erasing the pinched look that had been there. "Thanks for saying that. It means a lot."

"I'm completely serious," I said. "How much are you selling this for?"

"Two hundred," he said.

My jaw dropped. "That's way too low."

He shrugged. "I had it priced higher, but there was no interest, so I lowered the price."

"What was it originally?" I asked.

"Seven hundred."

"Still too low, but I'm not that much of an idiot to not take advantage of a good bargain," I said. "I'll take it for seven hundred."

His eyes went wide. "What do you mean, you'll take it?"

"I want to buy the bookshelf," I said.

"For what? I'm building you custom bookshelves for your library," he said.

"This is for my office downtown," I said. "It's the perfect look and size to display some of my authors' books."

"Jack," Connor said, "you don't have to buy this just because you feel sorry for me."

I stared blankly at him. "Why would I feel sorry for you?"

"Because I... never mind," he said. "But I don't need you buying furniture out of pity or some sort of weird obligation, all right?"

"I'm not," I said. I was starting to get pissed off but swallowed my anger down. "I'm buying the furniture because I want it. It has nothing to do with pity or obligation. Honestly, I'm a little insulted that you think it is."

Connor studied me for a moment. "Okay, well, thanks for purchasing the bookshelf."

"You're welcome." I could still hear the irritation in my voice. "Show me the nightstands."

I followed him around the maze of furniture, wishing I could take my time in studying each piece, but it was already close to seven, and I was sure Connor wanted to go home. Still, I couldn't help but stop when I saw the headboard leaning up against the wall.

I slipped past a dresser and another bookshelf and studied the headboard. It was even more gorgeous in person. I ran my fingers over the carvings of the vines and flowers etched into the wood. Connor joined me, and I said, "The detail in this is even more incredible in person."

"Thanks," Connor said. "It's my favourite piece. I just finished the matching footboard last Sunday."

"Shit, there's a footboard too?" I asked.

He nodded and moved a set of sturdy and functional looking kitchen chairs to the side to reveal the footboard. I crouched and studied it in the light from the overhead bulb. "Seriously, Connor, this is incredible. Do you mind if I take a picture of the two pieces?"

"No," he said.

I took out my phone and snapped a few pictures of each. "This is a queen size, yeah?"

"It is," he said.

"What's your asking price for these?"

He gave me a sharp look. "You have a king-size bed."

"It's not for me. However, I have a friend who I think would be interested."

"Oh. It's twenty-five hundred for the set."

I frowned. "That seems too low again."

He just shrugged as I tucked my phone away and followed him to the back of the storage unit. The nightstands were next to another set of kitchen chairs, these a bit more elaborate and expensive looking. "I like that you use a variety of wood and styles," I said. "It appeals to a broad range of people."

"Thanks. While I enjoy using the expensive shit for the furniture, I wanted to do some stuff that," he paused, "regular people could afford. Custom made furniture shouldn't just be for rich people."

I ran my hand along the top of the closest nightstand. "These are gorgeous."

Connor crouched and opened the drawer. "No need to wrestle the drawer open for -"

He stopped abruptly, his face turning a delightful shade of pink. Unable to resist – fuck, I had missed him – I crouched next to him in the pretense of examining the open drawer a little closer.

I inhaled his scent, my cock growing stiff from the way our thighs brushed. "Go on, finish your sentence."

Connor cleared his throat, his gaze dropping to my mouth. "It'll make it easier to get the lube for the next guy who shares your bed."

I leaned closer. "What if I want it to be you again?"

A muscle flickered in his jaw. I considered whether I should lean in and lick that ticking muscle when Connor pressed his mouth against mine. Apparently, he wasn't quite finished with me after all. Inner Jack practically danced for joy. I cupped his head, kissing him heatedly, trying to show him exactly how much I'd missed him the last four days.

I slid my tongue into his mouth, groaning at his already familiar taste. He leaned closer, lost his balance, and fell against me. I grunted and fell on my back, refusing to relinquish my hold on Connor and dragging him down on top of me.

I grinned up at him, my hands sliding up and down his back through his thin t-shirt. "You okay?"

"Are you? I weigh close to two hundred pounds," he said.

He tried to sit up, and even though the cement floor of the storage unit was incredibly uncomfortable, I wouldn't let him go. Instead, we stared at each other, our erect cocks perfectly aligned. The feel of his body on mine brought a sense of peace I hadn't felt since he left my bed Sunday night.

"Come back to my place for dinner," I said.

"It's already after seven," he said.

"I'll order something fast and disgustingly unhealthy for us," I said.

His eyes lit up. "Like McDonald's French fries?"

I laughed. "Whatever you want."

He studied my mouth. "Just dinner?"

"I want more than just dinner, but I'll take whatever you'll give me."

"What happened to only one night of fun?" Connor said.

"I've changed my mind."

"So, two nights?"

I pinched his ass through his jeans. "I was thinking at least three."

"So, what you're saying is three nights of sex and free McDonalds French fries?" Connor said.

"I'll even throw in some chicken McNuggets if you're a really good boy," I said.

He arched one eyebrow before gently rubbing his dick against me. "What do I have to do to get these nuggets? Be specific."

I tugged his head down and whispered into his ear. He

groaned, and his pelvis thrust against mine. "Fuck, yeah. I definitely want to do that. No need for a nugget bribe."

I kissed his neck. "The nugget stock prices are going to plummet."

He laughed, then stood and helped me to my feet. "I'll bring the nightstands by the house tomorrow before I start work on the library. And we can arrange a time for me to bring the bookshelf to your office downtown."

"Perfect," I said before I squeezed his ass and pressed another kiss against his mouth. "I'll see you back at my place, okay?"

"All right."

"I HAVE NEVER SEEN SOMEONE ENJOY FRIES AND CHICKEN nuggets this much before." I watched as Connor dipped another nugget into the sweet and sour sauce and took a bite. The bliss on his face as he chewed slowly made me grin.

"Hey, you don't get a body like this by eating nuggets and fries," he said. "McDonald's French fries are my favourite food, and I haven't had them in one hundred and twenty-seven days."

I laughed and ate one of the salty fries sticking out of the red carton in front of Connor. "I'm surprised you don't have it down to the hours and minutes too."

He thought for a moment. "Six hours and forty-two minutes."

I went to sneak another fry, I'd finished mine almost ten minutes ago, and Connor's hand clamped down on mine. "Buddy, I love you, but you keep eating my fries, and we're going to have a problem."

A spark of excitement flamed in my belly at his words,

which was incredibly stupid because it was just a turn of phrase. Connor didn't love me. We barely knew each other.

"Who knew you'd be so vicious over sharing fries." I withdrew my hand. "You're usually so laid back."

He stuffed the last of his fries into his mouth, the look of bliss deepening as he chewed and swallowed. "Favourite food, Jack. Favourite food."

"Let me guess. You had a McDonald's birthday party every year when you were a kid," I teased.

"Nah," he said. "Even before Dad died, we never had a lot of money. He worked construction, and with six kids, his wages barely covered the basics, let alone any extras. So, we didn't eat out, not even at the fast-food places."

"How did he die?" I asked gently.

"Car accident. It was his and Ma's anniversary in a month, and he wanted to buy her a bracelet, an expensive one that he'd seen at a local store. He'd worked double shifts for a couple of weeks. He was driving home after one and fell asleep at the wheel."

"I'm so sorry." I reached across the island and took his hand.

He stared at the island countertop, tracing his free hand over the pattern in the granite. "Shepherd was at work. Ma couldn't call him and tell him. She was too upset. So, I called him, and... it was the worst fucking moment of my life. Shepherd worshipped Dad, and I worshipped Shepherd, and to hear him start crying on the phone was..."

He swallowed hard. I slid to the stool closest to him and put my arm around his shoulders, tugging him closer until he rested his head against me. "I'm sorry, Connor."

"Thanks. Sorry to bring the room down," Connor said.

"You haven't." I smiled at him when he straightened.

"It's getting late," Connor said.

My stomach dropped. He'd changed his mind. Telling myself not to be pathetic and beg, I said, "It's only nine."

"Yeah, but I wanted to pick up the nightstands before work tomorrow, so…"

I made myself smile at him. "Oh, right. Okay, well, thanks for having dinner with me. I enjoyed hanging out with you tonight."

He frowned. "I thought we were having sex?"

"You said you had to leave."

"No, I said it was getting late," Connor said. "That was code for, let's go to the bedroom and fuck."

Relief made me giddy. "Why not just say let's go to the bedroom and fuck?"

"I was trying to be subtle."

"I prefer blunt."

"Hey, Jack?"

"Yeah?"

"Let's go to the bedroom and fuck."

I laughed and slid off the stool, taking his hand as we walked toward the bedroom. "See how easy that was?"

The minute we were in the bedroom, I pushed Connor up against the wall and kissed him hard. He returned my kiss just as eagerly, sucking on my tongue when I pushed it into his mouth. Finally, we broke for air, and Connor rested his forehead against mine as he pulled at the knot on my tie, loosening it.

"You look fucking hot in a suit, by the way."

"Thank you," I said. "You look hot in…oh fuck!"

Connor had given up on my tie and shoved his hand down my pants. He rubbed my dick as he kissed my jaw and nipped at my earlobe. "I've thought about your dick all fucking week."

"He's thought about you too." I yanked at my tie and

pulled it over my head before unbuttoning my shirt. As each button revealed more of my chest, Connor peppered the exposed skin with soft kisses that made me shiver with anticipation. He licked my nipple, and I gasped, bucking forward until I had him trapped against the wall. He gripped my ass and squeezed tight as we kissed again.

"You're wearing way too many clothes," I said when we came up for air.

"So are you."

"Let's fix that." I stepped away and stripped. Connor watched appreciatively for a moment before taking off his clothes. I left my clothes on the floor and walked over to the bed, yanking open the nightstand drawer and grabbing the lube and condom.

When I turned around, I couldn't help but laugh. Connor had picked up my clothes and was laying them neatly across the top of the dresser. "What are you doing?"

"These are expensive," he said. "You shouldn't just leave them lying on the floor."

"I have, like, fifty suits," I said.

"Of course, you do, Mr. Billionaire," Connor said as he joined me at the bed.

"Mr. Multi-Millionaire, thank you," I said with a grin.

He rolled his eyes and climbed into bed. "Get over here, multi-millionaire, so that I can suck your dick."

"See," I said as I knelt on the bed beside Connor, "this is why you're my fav... fucking hell, that's so good, baby." I cupped the back of his head, watching as Connor sucked on my cock as he fisted the base of it. "Your hot mouth feels amazing."

He cupped my balls, playing gently with them, as I thrust in and out of his mouth. Connor's dick was impossibly hard and dripping with precum. My mouth watered, and I pulled out of Connor's mouth with a soft pop.

"What's wrong?" he said.

"Nothing. Lie on your side."

He did what I asked, and I stretched out beside him with my head next to his dick. Connor groaned happily when I took him into my mouth, sucking lightly on the tip and cleaning away the precum.

He shifted slightly, and then his hot, wet mouth was sliding back over my dick. I groaned and took Connor deeper to the back of my throat, sucking hard as he did the same to me. I couldn't deep throat, at least not the way Connor did, but I took as much of his thick cock as I could, using my tongue to tease as I sucked hard.

For long moments, our low groans and mutual sucking were the only sounds in the room. Shamefully, I was already growing close. My desire for Connor for the last four days felt like an out-of-control wildfire finally contained. When he pressed on my taint, I gasped around his thick cock and pulled back.

"Baby, if you keep doing that, I'm gonna cum in your mouth."

"Good," he said and took me deep again as he pressed firmly on my taint.

"Oh fuck!" My hand tightened around the base of his dick, and I sucked his cock with fresh energy. I wanted to drive Connor crazy like he drove me crazy. I wanted him to spend all day tomorrow thinking about nothing but how this moment felt. I wanted him to want me and only me for the rest of his life.

Connor's groans were growing louder, his sucking turning erratic. I sucked harder and faster as my balls tightened and the base of my spine tingled. I was determined to bring him into the abyss with me and make him lose control as I had.

His cry around my dick was muffled as his cock swelled in my mouth. His mouth closed impossibly tight around my dick, and the pressure on my taint as he pressed again sent me over the edge. With a low cry, I came hard just as Connor thrust his cock deep into my mouth and his delicious tasting cum filled my mouth. I repeatedly swallowed, my body shaking as I emptied myself into Connor's mouth, my hand gripping his cock and stroking rapidly to get every last bit of Connor into my mouth.

We collapsed on our backs, our breathing ragged and harsh in the silence of the bedroom, both our bodies still quivering from our release.

"Oh my God," Connor said in a low voice. "I've never managed simultaneous orgasms before."

"Me neither," I croaked before sitting up and turning around, so I was lying next to Connor. I rested my head on the pillow beside his, cupping his face and pressing a kiss against his mouth. "Thank you."

"You're welcome," he said with a small smile. I threw my arm and my leg over Connor, tracing my fingers in light circles over his ribs.

"Not ticklish, huh?" I said.

"Not really. You?"

I shook my head, my fingers tracing the scar I could feel just above his hip. "What's this from?"

"Fell off my bike when I was ten," he said.

The room was starting to get a little stuffy, and I reached for the remote on the nightstand. I hit the button, and the ceiling fan whirred to life, the breeze cooling the sweat from our bodies.

"I should probably go," Connor said.

I automatically pulled him closer. "Stay the night with me."

"You sure?"

I nodded. "Yes. I want you to stay, Connor."

Relief washed over me when he said, "I want to stay too."

"Good." I traced the scar just above his hip again. "Why had it been almost a year since you've been with someone?"

"Just too busy. I started Hayes Carpentry two years ago, and it's a lot of work running your own company." He grinned at me. "I'm preaching to the choir here, aren't I?"

I shrugged. "Yes and no. I'm lucky in that I have a team of people to help me run mine. I'm not a one-person show like you are. That's much more work."

"I don't plan on being a one-person show forever, that's for sure," Connor said. "But in the meantime, there isn't a lot of room for a relationship, or even just casual sex."

He ran his fingers down the bumps of my spine. "How come you aren't dating anyone?"

"I was doing the dating app thing for a while," I said, "but it wasn't going well."

Connor laughed. "How many weirdos did you meet?"

"Actually, not that many," I said. "Just no real chemistry with the guys I did date. Mark says it's because all lawyers and doctors are boring."

"Is that what you're looking for?" Connor had tensed a little. "A lawyer or a doctor?"

I tried to be careful in my wording. "It's been my experience that while there's a certain romanticism in the idea of two people with wildly different lives falling in love, the reality is that it rarely works out."

"So, you dated a guy with no money, and he was only interested in your money, huh?"

I jerked a little before pulling back and staring at Connor. "I... well, yes, actually. Am I that transparent about it?"

He shrugged. "It doesn't take a genius to read between the lines. Tell me what happened."

"There isn't that much to tell," I said. "His name was Justin. I met him at a coffee shop where he worked as a barista. We dated for nearly three years before I found out he was cheating on me. In the three years, I'd bought him a car, a motorcycle, paid off his mortgage, and paid for everything on the seven vacations we'd taken together."

I glanced at Connor. "I didn't care that I'd spent the money. I loved him, and I wanted to help him. But the whole three years we'd dated, while I was busy falling in love and imagining a life together, Justin was fucking any guy who caught his eye and plotting how much of my money he could take before I stopped being an idiot and caught on to what he was doing."

"You weren't an idiot," Connor said. "You trusted someone who took advantage of that trust."

"I guess. Anyway, what about you? Any stories of love gone horribly wrong?"

"My first love didn't turn out so hot," Connor said.

I leaned against the headboard. "What happened?"

"We started dating in high school and all through university. Well, Darryl went to university. I started working construction to save for university, but it didn't pan out."

"Why not?" I asked.

"It was expensive, and I didn't know exactly what I wanted to do. I didn't want to waste my time or my money, so I just never... went," Connor said. "Darryl graduated with his business degree in finance and joined a pretty well-known firm here in town. Frankford Financials."

"They were my financial advisors for a while."

"Not anymore?"

I shook my head. "No, they fucked up on something, and I dropped them. Continue with your story."

"Darryl was smart, so fucking smart, and he got noticed pretty quick by the partners. Within a year and a half, he was promoted to senior manager. His responsibilities increased, but so did his pay. A year after that, he was a junior partner. I was so proud of him."

"What happened?" I asked.

"Darryl had a new lifestyle, and I didn't fit into it anymore," Connor said. "I was too broke, too uneducated, too embarrassing to bring to work events. He used to love my family, we spent so much time with them, but eventually, he found them embarrassing too. He broke up with me, and that was it."

"I'm sorry," I said. "That wasn't fair of him."

Connor shrugged, but I could see the pain in his face as he said, "Life isn't fair. I'm glad Darryl's doing well. He works hard and deserves it. He has a house in this neighbourhood now. It was his dream when we were teenagers. He wanted the big house and the fancy car and money to burn."

"What was your dream?" I asked.

"I didn't know at the time," Connor said. "I had other more pressing concerns like making sure my family didn't fall apart because my dad was dead."

I laid back down with him and pulled him into my embrace. "I'm so sorry, Connor." I pressed a quick kiss on his mouth.

"Honestly, I'm probably a little dramatic. It was Shepherd who did all the work to keep our family together. If it hadn't been for him, I don't know what Ma would have done."

"You're close to him," I said.

"He's my best friend," Connor said. "One time, Darryl

and I were having dinner with a work colleague of his. Shepherd happened to show up at the restaurant to meet friends. He had just left the shop, and he was still wearing his coveralls, and there was grease on his hands. He stopped by our table to say hello, and the look on Darryl's face…"

Connor took a deep breath. "Darryl told me later that night that it was humiliating for a colleague to see him with someone who looked like Shepherd."

"What an asshole," I said.

"We got into a huge fight and broke up," Connor said. "Nearly a decade of being together, and it was over because I couldn't afford the same lifestyle he did, and he'd suddenly decided my family, who'd been nothing but kind to him, were an embarrassment."

I could hear the sadness in his voice, and I stroked his back. "He didn't deserve you, Connor."

He didn't reply. I pulled him in even closer. It was meant to be a gesture of comfort, but I could feel Connor's cock hardening and his hands skimmed down my back to squeeze my ass. I smiled at him. "It's getting late. Are you sure you wouldn't rather sleep? I know you wanted to get up early tomorrow."

"I'm fueled by salt and grease and nuggets," Connor said.

I laughed and nuzzled his neck. "I've heard rumours that nugget fueled sex is the best sex."

Connor slid his hand between us and stroked my cock. "Then get ready for the best damn sex of your life, Jack Walker."

CHAPTER 10

Connor

I stared into my mostly empty fridge before closing the door. I was hungry, starving, in fact, but I couldn't be bothered to figure out something to eat. I considered calling Shepherd to see if he wanted to grab a bite to eat with me before dropping onto my sofa and closing my eyes.

I needed to get out more. I needed to make more friends beyond my brother so that I wasn't spending the third Friday in a row sitting in my empty apartment feeling sorry for myself. I used to have more friends, a lot more, but, just like my sex life, I'd sacrificed those friendships in exchange for trying to live my dream. Too many weekends turning down invitations to go out in favour of building furniture in Shepherd's garage had left me lonely and practically friendless the last six months.

I should have been at Shepherd's garage tonight, building… something, anything. But until Jack, sales of my custom furniture were nil, even with advertising on Facebook and Kijiji, and it was demoralizing as hell. I had a storage unit full of furniture, and there was no sense in creating more until I sold more pieces. Building a website and thinking of more creative ways to advertise needed to be my top priority, but neither of those paid the bills or kept me from starving.

I rubbed at the back of my neck. I needed to stick to the plan – build my carpentry business up and then concentrate on my actual life dream. At this point, the minimal amount of advertising I'd done, plus the materials to build the furniture, had put me in the hole, and I couldn't even afford the yearly fee for a damn website.

My phone buzzed, and I checked the screen, smiling when Nora's name popped up.

I opened it and read her text.

Oh my God, seriously, dude, Jack is the best. Eva is so excited about tomorrow!

I frowned. What was Nora talking about?

What do u mean?

My phone rang, and I hit the answer button. "Nora, what are you talking about?"

"I gave Jack my cell number when he had dinner at Ma's last weekend. He just sent me a text and invited the whole family to go swimming at his place tomorrow," Nora said. "You didn't know?"

"I... no, I haven't talked to him much today."

After spending the night in his bed, I'd gotten up early to return to my apartment for a shower and change of clothes. By the time I'd returned to his place with the nightstands, Jack had left for the office. I hadn't heard from him since, and I couldn't fool myself into thinking it didn't matter.

"Oh! Well, we're going to his place tomorrow around one. Even Nan said she might swim." Nora laughed. "She's gonna wear her two-piece, she says. What did you do to piss off Jack into not inviting you to the swim party?"

"I didn't do anything," I said. "I haven't – hold on, I have another call."

I checked my screen, my heart thudding when I saw Jack's name. "Nora, I gotta go. Jack's on the other line."

"Bye, honey. I'm sure I'll see you tomorrow. Love you!"

I took a deep breath and answered Jack's call. "Hey, Jack."

"Hi, Connor. The nightstands look fantastic in the bedroom, thanks."

"You're welcome." I could tell Jack was on speaker, and it was confirmed when I heard the honk of a horn.

"Try driving the speed limit, asshole," Jack muttered.

"So, uh, how was your day?" I asked. Why did it feel so awkward?

"Busy," Jack said. "Did you get the e-transfer for the bookshelf and the nightstands?"

"I did. Thanks again."

"Are you busy right now?"

"Uh, no, not really."

"Great, do you mind if I drop by your place?"

I hesitated. My apartment was shit compared to Jack's place. "I could come by your house."

"I'm close to your neighbourhood," Jack said.

"How do you know where my neighbourhood is?"

"Your Nan mentioned it at dinner last week. If it's a bad time, I don't have to -"

"No, it isn't," I said quickly. My desire to see Jack outweighed the embarrassment of my apartment. "I'll text my address."

"Perfect, see you soon."

I spent the next ten minutes tidying up my already tidy apartment and telling myself not to freak the fuck out that a millionaire – excuse me, *multi-millionaire* – was about to see my crappy apartment.

By the time Jack buzzed my apartment, I was mostly calm. Sweaty as fuck, but calm. I buzzed him in and opened my door, smiling at Jack when he came off the elevator. "Hey."

"Hello." He stepped inside, and I closed the door behind him. Jack studied my place. "This is nice."

I snorted and squeezed by him to grab a couple of beers from the fridge. "Do you want a beer?"

"I'd love one." Jack was wearing a t-shirt and athletic shorts. I tried not to think about those long muscular legs wrapped around my waist, but it was a losing battle.

Jack took the beer and followed me from the tiny kitchen to the equally tiny living room. I sat on the couch, making sure I took the end that had the spring nearly poking through. Jack sat on the other end and took a drink of beer before grinning at me.

"Why do you look like the cat who swallowed the canary?" I asked.

He laughed. "Do I?"

"Yes."

"Two things – I invited your family over for swimming and a barbeque tomorrow afternoon. Are you free to come as well?"

"I am," I said. "That's nice of you, Jack, but I hope you didn't feel obligated to do that."

"I didn't. Why would I?" he said with a puzzled look.

I didn't reply. Jack leaned forward, his Cheshire cat grin widening. "I have a buyer for the headboard and footboard."

I paused with my beer halfway to my mouth. "What?"

"One of my authors, Julia Wilden. I showed her the

pictures today when she came by for a meeting, and she loved them. Bought them on the spot."

"What do you mean, bought them on the spot?" I asked.

"She paid for them right then and there," he said. "Here." He took his wallet out of his pocket, opened it, and handed me some bills.

I stared wide-eyed at the top bill, trying not to drop the beer I still held in my other hand. I'd never seen a thousand-dollar bill before. "What the actual fuck? She paid you in cash?"

Jack laughed. "She's a bit eccentric. Pays for almost everything in cash."

"And she just had twenty-five hundred dollars in her damn purse?"

"Actually," Jack stared cagily at me, "don't be upset, but I quoted her a different price."

I shuffled through the cash I held. "A different... holy fuck."

I had to set my beer on the coffee table. My hand was too shaky to hold onto it any longer. I spread the six bills down on the couch between us, staring in mute disbelief at each thousand-dollar bill. "She... she paid you six thousand dollars?"

"She paid *you* six thousand dollars," Jack said and then took a drink of beer like he hadn't just changed my fucking life.

"You told her they were six grand?" I stared wide-eyed at him. "Why would you do that?"

"Because twenty-five hundred was way too low for them," Jack said. "Not with the amount of time it took to build them. You underpriced them."

"But six thousand?" I knew I sounded like an idiot, but I

couldn't stop. "Six thousand dollars? She paid six thousand dollars."

"She thought it was a deal," Jack said. "I probably could have got her to pay eight."

I swallowed hard. "Jack, they're not – I mean, they aren't worth six grand. I appreciate what you've done, but when this author sees them in person, she won't -"

"She's going to think she really did get a deal," Jack said. "They're absolutely worth six grand, Connor. Julia wants to meet you. Are you available to personally bring the headboard and footboard to her place some time next week?"

"Uh, yeah," I said. "But why does she want to meet me?"

"She's redoing her summer cottage. I told her that you have more furniture you've built. She wants to see what you have and discuss the possibility of making her some custom pieces. Make sure you bring her pictures of what you have built already. I have a feeling she'll love that table and chair set – the more elaborate ones over on the left side of the storage unit."

"Jack, I… holy shit. Thank you," I said as I stared at the money between us. "I don't even know… saying thank you doesn't seem like enough for what you just did, but I don't… I mean it from the bottom of my heart."

Jack scooped up the money and set it on the coffee table next to my beer before scooting closer to me. "You're welcome, Connor. And the thank you is enough, but if you were interested in doing a little more, I have a great idea."

"Oh yeah? What's that?" I said as Jack placed his hands on my inner thighs and rubbed gently.

"I have a couple of suggestions," he said before leaning in and pressing a kiss against my mouth.

I groaned and slid my hand around the back of his neck, slanting my mouth over his and kissing him deeply. He moaned, and the sound sent shivers down my spine. I was addicted to the sound of Jack's moans. Hell, I was a Jack Walker addict, period.

He pulled back, his firm lips slightly swollen from my kisses. "No obligation, of course, but I've done nothing but think about you and your thick cock all fucking day. I could barely concentrate at work."

"Girl, same," I said.

Jack burst out laughing, and warmth flushed through my body. I loved the sound of his laugh.

"At least I don't have to worry about cutting off a thumb with a table saw because I'm distracted," Jack said. "It's probably best that we do fuck again, so you're not so distracted. I mean, for thumb saving purposes, of course."

"Oh, if it's for thumb saving purposes, then, yeah, we definitely should fuck," I said.

Jack leaned forward to kiss me. I squeezed the back of his neck gently, pulling him to a stop. "Do you ever bottom?"

"A couple of times in the past," he said. "Is that something you want, Connor? Your cock in my ass?"

I groaned, my nostrils flaring and my cock turning into hard and throbbing stone behind my jeans. "Fuck, yes. So much, baby."

"Then take me to your bedroom." Jack stood and pulled on my hand. I stood and led him to my small bedroom, trying not to be embarrassed by the fact that it was so small I had to have my double bed pushed up against one wall.

"The bed is just a double," I said.

He smiled, his hands already busy unbuttoning my jeans. "That's cool." He slipped his hand inside my pants, his talented fingers driving me crazy with just a few strokes. "You have condoms and lube?"

"In the nightstand."

"Good." He kissed my chest through my t-shirt. "You're wearing too many clothes again."

"That seems to happen a lot around you," I said.

He nipped my neck. "I can't help it if I appreciate the beauty of your naked body."

I circled my hand over his crotch, rubbing the hard length of his cock through his shorts. "You sure about this?"

"This in general, or this meaning you fucking me?" Jack said.

"Both?"

"The answer is a very firm yes to both," Jack said. "Why are we still talking? This is the part where we undress and start fucking."

"So impatient," I said before pulling his shirt over his head. He returned the favour, and we helped each other finish undressing before Jack laid down on my bed. He grinned at me, one hand rubbing his perfect dick with slow strokes as I grabbed a condom and the lube.

I laid next to him, tracing my hand over his chest as we kissed. Fuck, I loved the way Jack kissed. Slow and deliberate, like he had all the time in the world to do nothing but precisely this.

"Connor," Jack breathed against my mouth, "grab the lube before I lose my damn mind."

I twisted my hand lightly up and down his cock. "It's early still. We have plenty of time."

"No," he said with a soft groan. "I need you, and I don't want to wait."

I thought about teasing him a little longer, but truthfully, I couldn't wait either. Not when I was so close to being in Jack.

I rolled to my other side, putting on the condom before slicking my cock with lube. Jack was kissing his way down my spine, and I shuddered and moaned when he licked the small of my back before biting my ass cheek.

"This ass," he said. "It's goddamn perfect. It deserves a billboard."

I laughed and flipped over to face him. "You want to put my ass on a billboard?"

"Yeah," he said as he kissed my chest and then sucked on my nipple.

I arched into him, trying not to be distracted by how fucking good it felt to have his hot mouth on me. My hands unsteady, I added lube to my fingers before reaching around Jack. He tensed when he felt my fingers against his hole. I kissed him and sucked on his bottom lip before saying, "Relax, baby. I won't hurt you, all right?"

He nodded, and I smiled in satisfaction when his body relaxed against mine. He buried his face in my throat, letting me explore and circle his hole with a light touch. He moaned when the tip of my finger slipped into him.

"Okay?" I said.

"Yeah. It feels good."

I slid my finger in further, my cock stiffening in anticipation at how tight Jack was. When I added another finger, Jack tensed for only a few seconds before relaxing again. "Good, baby," I said. "Stay nice and relaxed for me."

I stretched him, taking my time in doing it. The last thing I wanted to do was hurt him. I searched for his prostate, smiling a little when my finger brushed against it, and Jack's whole body twitched wildly. His precum coated my stomach, and he sucked in a breath. "Please, Connor."

"Maybe I should do that again," I said.

"Yes. Fuck, yes."

I rubbed his prostate with gentle strokes until he was moaning and pleading and thrusting his ass back onto my fingers. He whined in protest when I slid my fingers out. I kissed his chest. "Lie on your back, baby."

He relaxed on his back, watching through half-lidded eyes, with one hand stroking his dick as I added more lube to my cock and then massaged more into his tight hole. "You ready for me?"

"Hmm," he said, his free hand reaching up to tug at his nipple.

I kneeled between his legs and pressed on his knees until he raised his legs. Bracing them against his chest, I kept my hands on his shins as I stared at his gorgeous ass. "Spread your cheeks for me, honey."

He reached under his raised legs, his hands gripping his ass cheeks and pulling until he was open for me. I pressed the head of my cock against him, smiling reassuringly at him when he tensed again.

"Shh, no, honey, relax. I won't hurt you. I promise. I'll go nice and slow."

He took a deep breath, his body visibly relaxing as, still holding his legs up, I pushed forward. "Push against me, honey."

He pushed back, and we both groaned when the head of my dick slipped past the tight ring of muscle. "Fuck, that's so good," I muttered.

Jack blew out his breath. I waited patiently, even though every part of my body was screaming at me to take Jack and take him hard. He released a second deep breath. "I'm good."

I stroked his upper thighs as, inch by inch, I slowly moved forward until I was buried to the balls in Jack's tight ass.

"Fuck me, you're perfect," I moaned. "So tight and perfect."

I propped myself up on my hands above Jack, leaning

down so that we could kiss. He cupped the back of my neck, sliding his tongue deep into my mouth as he hooked his ankles at the small of my back.

"Okay?" I asked.

He nodded, and I made a few slow thrusts, trying not to blow my load at the feel of Jack's ass. Jack slid his arms around my waist, clinging tightly to me as I moved in and out of him.

"You feel so good," I said.

"You too," he gasped before bucking his hips a little. "Faster."

"You sure?"

"Fuck, yes," he groaned. "Move faster, Connor."

I raised myself a little more, enough that Jack could reach between us and stroke his cock as I fucked him. I watched his tanned hand move up and down his cock, squeezing and stroking as I thrust a little deeper, a little harder.

"Oh God," he moaned, his eyes closing and his head falling back as he touched himself. "Fuck, this feels good."

I shifted my body a little. Jack let his legs drop and then spread them wide. I loved his trust in me, loved that he knew I would never hurt him. I thrust back and forth, shifted my body again to try to aim for his prostate, and grinned when I made another thrust, and Jack groaned loudly.

His hand moved hard and fast over his cock, and I matched that rhythm, brushing against his prostate with every stroke of my dick.

"Oh fuck, oh fuck, oh fuck," Jack chanted. "I'm gonna cum. I'm gonna…"

His ass squeezed impossibly tight around my dick, making me cry out with pleasure and pulling my orgasm from me in an unstoppable wave of bliss. Cum spurted out of Jack's dick, splattering across his abdomen and chest as I pumped in and out of him with heavy strokes that made me shudder with pleasure.

My arms were shaking from exertion, and my legs were weak from my orgasm. I pulled out of Jack before I could fall on him and then eased off the bed. Jack sprawled on the bed, his eyes closed and his body quivering.

I disposed of the condom and wetted a cloth with warm water in the bathroom before returning to the bedroom. Jack was lying in the same position, and I admired the lean length of his body before sitting on the bed and cleaning off his stomach and dick.

"Thank you," he mumbled.

"You're welcome." I tossed the cloth in the hamper and climbed into bed beside him. He turned on his side, and I spooned him tight, kissing the back of his shoulder. "You okay? Did I hurt you at the end?"

"No," he said. "Not at all. I feel fantastic."

"Good."

When my stomach growled, Jack cracked open one eye and craned his head to stare at me. "Did you eat supper?"

"Not yet," I said.

"It's almost eight."

I didn't answer, and Jack rubbed my arm. "I haven't eaten either. Let's order sushi. Do you like sushi?"

"I do," I said.

"Thank God," he said with a slight grin. "Our relationship would suffer if you didn't."

Relationship?

I tried to ignore the hope flaring to life in my belly, but it was almost impossible. Jack had said he didn't want to date, but this felt a fuck of a lot like dating to me. I wasn't sure how I felt about that. Part of me was thrilled at the idea, but the other part? It knew exactly how bad of an idea that was.

"What do you say? Sushi for dinner?" Jack said. "My treat."

"Sure, but we can go back to your place if you want," I said. "I know it's... nicer."

He frowned at me. "There's nothing wrong with your place, Connor."

"Compared to your house, it's a piece of shit," I said.

"I like it. I know I haven't seen all of it, but it has its charms."

"Oh, you've seen all of it," I said. "It's a one-bedroom apartment. There isn't anything else to it."

Jack grinned at me. "I like your place, and I'm happy to spend the night here with you."

I blinked at him, and Jack flushed. "Shit, sorry. I'm being presumptuous about spending the night. I didn't mean -"

"It's all good," I said quickly before my brain could tell me what a dumb idea this was. "I want you to stay the night."

"Great." Jack gave me a quick kiss on the lips. "Now order me sushi before I'm too weak to fuck you later."

"Honey, I'm about to order so much sushi," I said and reached for my phone, Jack's laugh warming my entire body.

CHAPTER 11

Connor

"Daddy, catch me!" Eva jumped fearlessly into the pool, squealing excitedly when James caught her. He kissed her cheek and watched her paddle in the water. Angie and her husband, Rob, were on the float together. Eva laughed when they floated by, and Rob splashed a bit of water on her.

"Uncle Davey, do another handstand!" Eva shouted.

Davey grinned at her and dipped under the water. Eva clapped her hands in excitement when his feet and lower legs popped up out of the water.

Tristan and Shepherd sat on the edge of the pool, deep in conversation, with their feet dangling in the water.

"Uncle Shepherd, get in the pool with us," Eva called.

"In a minute, Eva," Shepherd said.

"It's so nice of Jack to invite us all for a pool party, isn't it, dearest?" Nan smiled at me. She wore a two-piece bathing suit, a giant sunhat, and oversized sunglasses that gave her the look of a glamorous movie star.

"Yes," I said. "Very nice."

Ma sipped at her glass of wine before lying back on the lounger. "I haven't felt this relaxed in forever. Jack's house is just lovely. He showed me your work on the library, honey. It looks fantastic. I'm so proud of you."

"Thanks, Ma."

"It looks almost finished," she said.

"It is, just another couple of weeks to finish up, I think." I glanced over to the outdoor kitchen. Jack had just brought out a tray of burgers and hot dogs. I stood up from the lounger and joined him. "What can I do to help?"

He smiled at me. "Nora's grabbing the other lunch stuff from the kitchen. You could help her bring it out."

Nora walked out of the house with two large bowls of salad. She wore a bright pink bathing suit that matched the colour of her hair, and, like Nan, she wore oversized sunglasses. She set the salads on the table. "Swimming *and* lunch... Jack, you're spoiling us."

Jack laughed. "It's just burgers and hot dogs."

"Still, it's so -"

"Hey, sorry, I'm late. Traffic was a nightmare."

I turned at the sound of Mark's voice. He walked toward us as Nora turned around. She gasped and clawed her sunglasses off her face as Mark stopped next to us. She stared wordlessly at him as he held out his hand. "Hi, I'm Mark."

"You... you're Mark Reynolds," Nora said. "You're an author. A really good author."

"My mom thinks so," Mark said with a small smile.

He was still holding his hand out, and I nudged Nora when she didn't move. She blinked at me before turning back to Mark. After a few more seconds, I said, "Mark, this is my sister, Nora. She's a big fan."

Nora twitched before taking Mark's hand and pumping it

rapidly. "Not just a big fan, your number one fan. I'm obsessed with you and your books, Mr. Reynolds."

Her eyes widened. "I sound like I'm going to hold you captive in my cabin in the dead of winter and cut off your foot with an axe. I won't. I swear I won't. I don't even have a cabin. Just a studio apartment. And no axe. I definitely don't have an axe. I have mace. Not that I'm going to use the mace on you, because I definitely won't use the mace on you. I just have it for... oh God, why am I still talking? Why can't I stop talking?"

She turned to me and whispered, "Connor, make me stop talking."

"Give the nice man his hand back, Nora," I said.

With an eep of embarrassment, she dropped Mark's hand. "Shit, I am so sorry. Shit! I should not be saying shit."

"Three dollars, Auntie Nora!" Eva hollered from the pool.

Mark laughed. "It's nice to meet you, Nora. And if it makes you feel better, I say shit all the time. Also, call me Mark."

Nora swallowed hard. "Mark. Hi, Mark."

"Hi, Nora," Mark said.

Jack stared at Mark and Nora with a look of amusement. "Nora, you and Mark grab beers and relax. Connor will help me with lunch, won't you, Connor?"

"Yes," I said.

Her eyes still wide and her hands shaking, Nora took the beer Mark offered her from the cooler. She gripped it tightly as Mark pointed to the empty loungers near Ma and Nan. "Why don't you introduce me to the rest of your family?"

"Of course, right, yes, I'll introduce you to the rest of my family," Nora said. Her gaze star-struck, she followed Mark toward Ma and Nan.

Jack grinned at me when we were alone. "That was hilarious."

"Jack... you invited Mark so Nora could meet him?"

"Yes. I mean, Mark and I are friends, so it's not that weird to invite him over for food, but I thought it would make Nora happy to meet him."

"You're amazing," I said. I was getting a little choked up, but I didn't care how it looked to Jack. "I... what you just did for Nora... she'll never forget this, Jack. You have no idea what this moment will mean to her."

"I'm glad I could do something special for her." Jack reached for the burgers, and I grabbed his hand and pulled him into my arms.

He made a startled oof when I pressed my mouth against his. I didn't care that my family was right there, didn't care if they were watching. I slipped my arms around his waist and kissed him until he made a low moan and returned my kiss.

When I finally released his mouth, he blinked at me a couple of times. "That was... unexpected."

"I want more," I said.

"Me too, but if you keep kissing me like that, we're gonna have a problem with inappropriate erections," he said with a grin.

"No, I mean I want to date you," I said.

The shock was written all over his face. Before I could lose my nerve, I said, "Look, I know it's a bad idea, okay? You're basically my boss, and we have very little in common, but I like you. I like you a lot. I know I'm not a lawyer or a doctor, but I swear I'm not interested in your money. I'm interested in you because you're funny and smart and so damn hot. I think we could be terrific together. Will you give us a chance?"

"You have to date Uncle Connor," Eva said.

Jack and I both looked down. Eva, water dripping from her tiny body, grinned at us. She held Mr. Perkins in one hand and her water wings in the other. "He's my favourite uncle. Also, you're rich, and you curse, so I can make a lot of money off of you."

Jack burst into hard laughter. I grinned at him. "I mean, you kind of have to date me now. Eva said so."

Jack pressed a kiss against my mouth. "I like that you have a six-year-old as your wingman."

"Seven," Eva said.

"Six and three quarters," James yelled from the pool.

We turned to see my entire family and Mark staring at us.

"Well?" Angie said. "Are you two dating or not?"

"We are," Jack said, making me grin like a fool and my heart bang against my ribcage.

"Thank fuck," Angie said.

"Language," James said.

"You owe me a dollar, Auntie Angie," Eva said.

"Worth it," Angie said.

I turned back to Jack, keeping my arm around his waist, and pressed another kiss against his mouth. He pulled me closer and whispered into my ear, "Don't take this the wrong way, but I can't wait for your family to leave. I want you naked and in my bed."

I grinned at him. "I was thinking the same thing."

Jack

"If I run face-first into a wall, I'm blaming you," I said.

Connor laughed, keeping his arm tight around my waist

as he guided me down the hallway. "I'm not going to run you into a wall, Jack. Keep your eyes closed."

"They're closed," I said.

"Good. Okay, we're in the library. Don't peek. Keep them closed!"

"They are," I said with a laugh as Connor turned my body in the opposite direction. For the last week, he hadn't let me set foot in the library. Finally, he'd finished the final touches this morning, and I couldn't wait to see it completed.

"Okay, ready?"

"Yes," I said. "I'm dying over here, Connor."

"Open your eyes."

I blinked them open, staring in mute amazement at my new library. Connor had faced me in the reading room's direction, and I studied the two columns and the small room beyond it before turning in a slow circle and exploring the entire room.

"Well? What do you think?" Connor's voice was nervous.

"Oh my God," I said. "Connor, it's…"

"It's what?" he said, his usual low voice pitched higher than normal.

"It's perfect," I said. "Absolutely perfect."

Connor released his breath, and the tight grip on my waist loosened a little. "You sure you like it?"

I cupped his face and kissed him. "Not just like… I love it, Connor. I can't wait to fill the shelves with my books. It's going to look exactly as I'd pictured my library would look."

I kissed him again before wandering the room, admiring the floor-to-ceiling bookshelves and the two rolling ladders before I stepped into the sectioned-off reading room. I sank into one of the chairs as Connor sat in the opposite one.

"This is perfect," I said. "The coffee table looks fantastic in here."

Connor grinned. "Not to sound immodest, but it really does."

"I can't wait to show Mark," I said. "He'll be so jealous. He'll probably hire you to build his library."

"Hey, I'm all for it," Connor said. "But first, I need to finish Judy and William's pool house. Thank you again, by the way, for the recommendation."

"You're welcome," I said. "There's a homeowner's association meeting next month, and I plan on showing everyone pictures of my new library. I think you can expect to get a few more jobs from it."

I loved the pleased look that crossed Connor's face. In the last two weeks, I'd discovered just how easy it was to make him happy, and, honestly, nothing made *me* happier. It wasn't just about spending money on him either. An unexpected back rub, taking his Nan out for coffee, hanging a swing on the apple tree so Eva could use it... all of those small and insignificant things brought that same look of happiness to Connor's face. I could spend the rest of my life making Connor Hayes happy.

Connor's phone buzzed, and he glanced at the screen before shaking his head and laughing. When he finished texting, I said, "What was that about?"

"That was Nora. She's having lunch with Mark today."

"Again?" I said. "Those two have been inseparable since they met."

"They really clicked," Connor said. "Shepherd said Ma told him Mark is coming to family dinner this weekend."

"That's awesome," I said as my phone buzzed. I checked the screen and cursed under my breath before shoving it back into my pocket.

"What's wrong?" Connor said.

"Just some more issues with that author I mentioned

before. She won't shut the fuck up on social media, and she's making everything worse. It's a problem I need to deal with but not at this very moment. Did you talk to James about Eva's birthday present?"

Connor leaned back in the chair. "I did. He said he doesn't want you to feel obligated, but yes, he is one hundred percent okay with you buying Eva the Barbie car for her birthday."

"Great. I'll have my assistant pick it up," I said. "When do you start the pool house job?"

"Not until the week after next. They have family in town next week," Connor said. "But we've already gone over exactly what they want, and they've signed the contract, so we're good to go. I can use the week off to get started on the custom furniture pieces that Julia ordered."

"I knew she'd order more," I said.

Connor grinned at me, the excitement on his face shining out like the brightest light. "She ordered custom nightstands, a credenza, and a cabinet for her good china. I quoted her a price, and she didn't even blink. Just told me to send the invoice to her PA, and she'd get it paid."

"She understands that amazing quality like your work costs money," I said. "Listen, I've been thinking a lot about this lately… you should open up a store space for your furniture."

"It's a great idea and one I want to do in the future, but not right now," Connor said.

"Why not?" I asked. "Connor, your furniture is crazy good, and I know so many people who would purchase it. But, at the very least, you need to get a website up and running for it. I'd like to show off your furniture at the homeowner's association meeting but trust me – these people are snobs. A few pictures in a storage unit won't cut it. But if you hire a professional to take some pictures of the furniture, set up a website with the pictures and your pricing – I have a feeling you'll get a ton of sales."

"I appreciate that," Connor said, "but I just don't have the time right now for all of that."

"You have a week between jobs," I said. "You could hire a photographer and a website designer to get it done."

"It's not a good time," Connor said.

"What better time than now?" I said. "Connor, this is your dream, right? It's not going to happen if you're just sitting on your ass. You need to put in the effort and -"

"Put in the effort?" Connor's face was turning red, and I realized too late that I hadn't just upset him. I had royally, majorly, pissed him off.

"I run my own company with zero help. I'm trying to build this company which means long hours and hustling my ass off every minute of every day, so don't tell me I'm not putting in the effort," Connor said.

"I apologize," I said. "I know you work hard, Connor, I do. But my point is that you're working hard to build a company that ultimately isn't your dream. Why do that when you can do what you really love?"

"Because this job is a hell of a lot more stable than custom furniture building," Connor said. "Hayes Carpentry is a need for people. Hayes Custom Furniture is a want. So, at this point, I can't take the risk."

"Life is about risk," I said. "You're too good at building furniture to waste your time doing something else. You can do this, Connor."

He shook his head, his face still red and his knee bouncing up and down in a jittery motion. "I don't have the money to open a store right now."

"You could get a loan from the bank," I said. "As long as you have some -"

"It's not that simple," Connor said. "I don't have banks dying to give me money like they are with you."

I was starting to get irritated at his excuses. "Have you ever spoken to a bank about it? You can't just assume they won't give you a loan."

Connor scoffed. "Jack, get your head out of the clouds. They're not going to give me a loan."

"You don't know that," I said. "Why are you making excuses? If you really want this, you'll find a way to -"

"If I really want this?" Connor stood up, his hands clenched in fists and his body nearly vibrating with anger. "If I really want this, Jack? You have money practically falling out of your ass, and you have no idea what it's like for people in the real fucking world. So, don't you dare tell me that the only reason I'm not doing what I love for a living is that I don't *want* it enough."

"Connor, I'm sorry, I didn't mean -"

"You did," Connor said. "You did mean it, Jack."

We stared silently at each other before Connor started toward the door. "I gotta go. I'll talk to you later."

I slumped in my chair, staring out the window as the front door slammed, and I heard the dim roar of Connor's truck starting.

Shit. I'd really fucked up.

"I TOOK A DEEP BREATH AND KNOCKED ON CONNOR'S apartment door. A week after we'd started dating, he'd given me a key to the building and his apartment. I'd let myself into the building but knowing how pissed Connor was at me this morning, I wasn't comfortable just walking into his apartment.

The seconds ticked by, and I started to wonder if Connor would even let me in. I knocked again, my heart a jittery erratic thumping in my chest and sweat sliding down my back. What if I'd fucked up so much that Connor never wanted to see me again?

I was about to knock a third time when the door opened, and Connor, soaking wet and wearing just a pair of shorts with a towel over one beefy shoulder, stared silently at me.

I swallowed hard, ignoring the way my cock stirred at the sight of Connor's tanned wet skin. I held up the pizza box and the six pack of beer. "I brought pizza, beer, and an apology."

Connor stepped back. "Come in."

I stepped inside, shutting the door with my foot before following Connor to the kitchen. I set the pizza and the beer on the table and sank into one of the chairs. Connor used the towel to dry his hair and upper body before tossing it on the sofa.

"Sorry for interrupting your shower," I said.

He sat down across from me and twisted off the cap on one of the beers. He took a long drink, nearly half the bottle, before setting it back on the table.

"I'm sorry, Connor," I said. "I stepped way over the line earlier today. I shouldn't have pushed you the way I did, and I promise that I know and understand how incredibly hard you work. I pushed you because I want you to be happy, but I stuck my nose into a place it didn't belong. It was wrong of me, and I sincerely apologize. It won't happen again."

He sighed and rubbed the back of his neck. "Thank you. I'm sorry for getting so pissed off. I shouldn't have stormed out like a toddler having a temper tantrum."

"That's okay," I said. "I was talking out of my ass, and you didn't need to put up with that."

He smiled at me, and relief swept through me. Maybe I hadn't completely fucked my relationship with Connor after all.

"I appreciate the apology," he said. "And the beer and the pizza."

"I guessed that you'd completely lost your appetite like I had and hadn't eaten dinner yet," I said.

"It was a good guess," he said.

There was silence between us that wasn't wholly awkward but not entirely comfortable either.

"I guess that was our first fight," I said.

"I guess so," he said.

"I got your favourite – pepperoni and bacon," I said. "We should eat while it's still hot."

"I've always been a fan of cold pizza," Connor said.

I smiled a little. "Is that right?"

"Yeah," Connor said. "I mean, we just had our first fight, so technically, shouldn't we be having our first round of make-up sex?"

"It does seem to be the rules," I said. "And I'm a stickler for the rules."

Connor stood and held out his hand. I took it, and he pulled me to my feet before giving me a hard and deep kiss that made my dick hard and my entire body shiver.

I sucked on his bottom lip before resting my forehead against his. "Take me to your bedroom. We'll let the pizza cool down while we have super hot, sort of angry, make-up sex."

Connor laughed. "Sounds like the perfect Tuesday night."

I took his hand and kissed his knuckles before following him to his bedroom.

CHAPTER 12

Connor

"Best trip to the aquarium ever," Eva announced. "Let's do it again next Friday."

Angie groaned. "Sweetheart, I love you, but I'm not spending every Friday night at a watery zoo with my entire family."

Davey stared at her in mock outrage. "The newlywed doesn't want to spend all her free time with her family? I, for one, am delighted to spend every Friday night with the family I love and adore. Which is why I'm Ma's favourite."

"Bullshit, you're Ma's favourite," Nora said. "I am."

"One dollar!" Eva hollered.

"Excuse me?" Shepherd was holding hands with Tristan as we walked back to the parking lot.

"Don't even, Shepherd," Angie said as Nora handed a dollar bill to Eva. "You can't be Nan's favourite *and* Ma's favourite. Just let this one go."

"She's right, dearest," Nan said. "You'll have to be happy just being my favourite."

"Nan!" Angie stared at her. "You're not supposed to actually say he's your favourite."

Nan had her arm hooked around Rob's, and she grinned up at him. "Your wife is adorable. You know that, right?"

"I do," Rob said with an affectionate look at Angie. "Hey, can a Hayes kid by marriage throw his hat in the ring for favourite kid? Because I brought Alison her favourite caramel fudge last week, so I think I might be in the running."

"Absolutely not," Nora said. "Besides, it doesn't matter because I am, without a shred of doubt, Ma's favourite. Right, Ma?"

"I don't have a favourite child," Ma said. "But if I did, obviously it would be James."

Shepherd and I both burst into laughter as James grinned at Nora. She clapped her hand to her chest and announced in a tone one might hear from an actor going hard for an Oscar. "Betrayed by my own mother."

"It's a shame that Jack couldn't join us," Nan said. "Is everything going all right with him, dearest?"

I nodded as I opened Ma's car door and helped Nan slide into the front seat. "Yes. He had plans with Mark tonight."

"Is he coming for dinner on Sunday?" Nan said.

"He'll be there."

"Oh, good." Nan patted my cheek when I carefully drew the seatbelt across her and clicked it into place. "Thank you, dearest."

"You're welcome, Nan."

Mom opened her car door. "Okay, so everyone knows where Savory Fusion is?"

"Why can't we go to Chuck E Cheese?" Eva said as James picked her up and opened the back door to his SUV. "We always go to Chuck E Cheese."

"Which is why we're going to Savory Fusion this time.

It's a new restaurant that Grandma's wanted to try for a long time," James said.

"But I love Chuck E Cheese," Eva said.

"I know," James said, "but sometimes adults like to have a meal in a restaurant that doesn't have a giant ball pit in the middle of it."

"Man, I'm never gonna be an adult," Eva said as James sat her in her car seat and buckled her in.

Nora threw her arm around my waist. "Can I catch a ride with you to the restaurant? Angie and Rob are still in their honeymoon phase, and Shepherd and Tristan are also disgustingly gaga with each other. It's gross."

"You're welcome to join me in my Fortress of Solitude," I said.

She laughed. "Oh please, if Jack were here, I'd be begging Davey for a ride because the two of you are as disgustingly, adorably gross as the others."

I slung my arm around her shoulders and kissed the top of her head. "We really are."

"OH DEAR," MA SAID AS THE ELEVEN OF US STOOD IN THE foyer of the restaurant. "Maybe we should go somewhere else for dinner."

"Why?" Nora said.

"This place is a little fancier than I thought," Ma said. She studied the hostess, who wore what looked like an evening dress and four-inch heels.

"It's fine," Angie said.

"We don't exactly fit in with the rest of the customers," I said.

Angie scowled at me. "So what? They're not better than

us just because they wear expensive clothes."

"The menu wasn't that expensive when I looked at it online," Ma said, "so I didn't think it would be this fancy. I'm fine with trying something else."

"No, you're not," Davey said. "You've been talking about this place for months, Ma."

"I know, but…"

"We already have the reservation booked," James said. "It's all good, Ma."

"Are you sure?" Ma said.

"We're eating here," Shepherd said with finality. He smiled at the hostess as she approached us. She gave him and his tattoos a decidedly nervous look.

"Good evening. Do you have a reservation?"

"We do," Angie said. "It's under Hayes."

The hostess checked her tablet before nodding. "Of course, right this way."

"THIS RESTAURANT WAS A GREAT IDEA, ALISON," TRISTAN said. "The food is delicious." He set his cutlery on his empty plate before taking Shepherd's hand.

"I thought they had a pretty varied vegan section on their menu," Alison said.

"They did," Shepherd replied. "Thanks for thinking of us, Ma."

"Of course, honey."

"Daddy? I ate everything on my plate. Can I have dessert?" Eva said.

James smiled at her. "You bet, Bunnykins." He leaned down and kissed her forehead. "Thank you for being so well-behaved during dinner. I'm very proud of you."

"I'm almost seven, Daddy," Eva said. "I know how to behave in a fancy restaurant."

We all laughed as Eva grinned and said, "But I wouldn't say no to a trip to Chuck E Cheese tomorrow night."

"Nice try," James said, "but I think eating out once this week is more than enough."

Eva leaned back in her chair. "If I weren't saving up for a Barbie car, I'd treat us both to Chuck E Cheese, Daddy."

"That's very generous of you," James said with a grin at me.

"I know. I'm a generous -" Eva's eyes widened, and she let out a screech of happiness that made everyone sitting near us turn to look at her. "Jack! It's Jack! Jack's here!"

Before James could stop her, she slid from her chair, raced halfway across the restaurant, and skidded to a stop at a table near the window. I automatically stood as James stood up.

"I'll get her," I said.

I weaved my way around tables. The excited squeals of Eva echoed through the restaurant as she danced in front of Jack's table. "Jack! Hi! What are you doing here? Who's this lady? Uncle Connor said you were with Mark. Why aren't you with Mark? We went to the aquarium tonight! I got a dolphin tattoo! Look!"

I cringed when she yanked up her shirt and showed Jack the temporary tattoo Nora had plastered across her stomach. I joined them, smiling apologetically at Jack and the woman he was with as I tugged Eva's shirt down. "Sorry about this."

"Everyone's here, Jack!" Eva grabbed Jack's hand and grinned at him. "The whole family! Look!"

Jack gave her a distracted smile. "That's nice, Eva."

"Look! You're not looking!" she said in a loud voice before tugging on his hand again.

"Eva, enough," I said.

Jack, his face red and his entire body tense, gave me a small and painfully formal grin. "Hello, Connor."

"Hi," I said. "Sorry to interrupt."

His smile turned to a grimace as he glanced at the woman sitting across from him. "Mary Crawford, this is Connor Hayes."

"Nice to meet you." The woman barely looked at me.

I wasn't surprised. She practically dripped with diamonds, and the shirt she wore looked like real silk. She studied Eva with obvious disdain, and my back prickled.

I cleared my throat as Eva squeezed Jack's hand again. Her voice still a loud and excited pitch, she said, "I saw the coolest thing at the aquarium today, Jack. It was a baby -"

"That's nice, Eva," Jack said. "I'm glad you had a nice time at the zoo." He pulled his hand free and gave me a look that clearly said, *leave right the fuck now*, before staring at the woman sitting across from him.

Eva deflated before my eyes. "It was the aquarium, not the zoo."

I picked Eva up and set her in the crook of my arms. "Good to see you again, Jack."

He made a distracted wave, his gaze still on Mary.

Sick to my stomach, my cheeks practically on fire, I turned and strode across the restaurant, too aware of the way the other customers were watching us.

"Why was Jack acting that way?" Eva said. "Did I say something bad, Uncle Connor?"

"No, sweetie, you did nothing wrong. I promise."

I sat her in her seat before sitting down in my seat next to Shepherd. I stared at my plate as Angie said, "I thought Jack was with Mark tonight."

"Angie," Ma said gently.

"What?" Angie said. "We know he's not, like, having an affair with the chick. He's gay, not bi. So why did he lie to Connor?"

"Enough, Angie," Shepherd said.

"I think I'll try the chocolate mousse for dessert," Nan said in a loud voice. I was grateful to her for the change of subject. I stared listlessly at the dessert menu in front of me as everyone else discussed the dessert options.

Shepherd leaned in close. "You okay, buddy?"

"Yes," I said.

"I'm sure Jack has a good reason for why he isn't with Mark," Shepherd said.

"Yeah, probably."

Shepherd gave me a sympathetic look. I didn't know how to tell him that Jack lying to me about his plans tonight was the last thing I cared about. That it wasn't the lies making me feel like I was about to vomit, but the way he blew us off, and the obvious shame he felt at knowing a family like us once he was with other people of his social status. It was Darryl all over again, and the realization that Jack was exactly like him sent me into a spiral of anger and sorrow and regret.

"WE NEED TO TALK." I SAT DOWN AT THE ISLAND IN JACK'S kitchen.

After finishing dinner, I'd gone back to my apartment and stewed for nearly two hours before driving to Jack's place. I stared at him as he blew out his breath in a harsh sigh. He was still wearing his suit, with the tie pulled loose and the top buttons of his collar undone. He looked exhausted physically and mentally, but my anger wouldn't let me care.

"I know," he said, "but can I take a quick shower first and -"

"No," I said, "this can't wait. Tonight, at the restaurant -"

"I didn't lie about my plans with Mark," he said quickly. "I had plans with him but then -"

"I don't care about that," I snapped. My anger was a raging inferno inside me.

I stood and paced back and forth in front of the island. "You know, you had me fooled. I thought you were different from Darryl. I really did. But I was so fucking wrong."

"What are you talking about?" Jack asked.

I laughed bitterly. "Of course, you don't even know. Why would you?"

"Connor, I know you're pissed because you think I lied to you, but I didn't -"

"I don't care that you lied to me!" I shouted. "You blew me off! Hell, you blew Eva off in that restaurant! You were ashamed to be seen with us. Because you're exactly like Darryl. You say all the right things when it's just us, and you act like you don't fucking care that I'm poor, but in the end, rich people are all the same. Get them in a room together, and they look at people like me like we're nothing. Like we don't matter because we don't have fat bank accounts or -"

"Stop it!" Jack roared.

Caught off guard by the anger in his voice, I staggered back, staring silently at him as he stood and pounded his fist on the island. "You asshole, Connor. You won't give me a chance to explain. You just walk in here and accuse me of being an entitled, arrogant prick without even knowing the circumstances of the evening. I'm sorry that I've upset you, but do you have any idea the fucking shitty night I've had?"

"You've had a shitty night?" I said. "How awful for you. Did your boyfriend act like he was ashamed to know you?

Act like he didn't give a fuck about you just because he was
-"

"I was in a goddamn work meeting!" Jack shouted. "That woman with me? She's one of my authors, a woman who I've worked with for a very long time. But she fucked up, Connor."

I stared blankly at him as he grimaced and said, "She said something incredibly inappropriate on social media a few weeks ago. Do you remember me telling you that?"

"Yes," I said.

"We've been in constant damage control mode since. And she certainly hasn't made it fucking easy for us. You have no idea how many hits Walker Publishing has taken in the last few weeks, how many fires I've had to put out because one fucking author can't keep her fucking mouth shut. Earlier today, she posted on social media again with another derogatory and homophobic comment that wasn't just a step over the line. It was a giant fucking leap. Then she spent the entire day doubling down on her comment and enraging half the fucking book community in the meantime."

"Shit," I said.

He laughed bitterly. "Shit? Yeah, that's putting it mildly. The shitstorm I have had to wade through today, the apology statements I've had to draft and draft again, all while Mary fucking Crawford keeps running her fucking mouth all over social media. I called the meeting tonight because I was dropping her as a client."

He raked a hand through his hair, his frustration palpable. "She refused to take my calls or to come to the office. She made me meet her in a public place because she was just stupid and arrogant enough to think I wouldn't fucking fire her and make a scene."

I swallowed hard. We had left before Jack and the

woman, so I had no idea what happened between them. "Did you?"

"Yes," he said. "Then had to deal with Mary freaking the fuck out in the restaurant, screaming and crying, and threatening to sue me and my entire fucking company. I'm sorry that I was distracted and hurt your feelings, but I can assure you that my blowing you off had nothing to do with your family or your socio-economic status."

"I'm sorry," I said. "Jack, I didn't know."

"No, you didn't," he said. "But you didn't even give me the benefit of the doubt, did you? You went straight to the worst possible scenario in your head. You made me into the bad guy, made me exactly like Darryl, because deep down inside, you truly believe I am exactly like your dick of an ex-boyfriend. It doesn't matter that I clearly love your family and spending time with them. Hell, it doesn't even matter that it's obvious I am completely and madly in love with you. You see what you want to see in me. A rich prick who's never going to accept you for who you are."

"I'm sorry," I repeated. "You're right."

He sat down with a weary thump, like a balloon that had lost all of its air. "I was hurt in the past too, Connor. I was cheated on and used for my money, but I still saw you for who you really were. I didn't and never will compare you to Justin because I believed you when you told me who you were. But you," he shook his head, "you won't even give me a chance to prove to you that I'm not like your ex."

"I will," I said. "Jack, I made a mistake. A massive one, but you have to see it from my point of view."

It was the wrong thing to say. I knew it immediately. But, hell, I was panicking, and my anger had left, leaving me feeling sick to my stomach at the thought of losing Jack.

"Your point of view, huh? The one where I'm nothing but

a rich asshole who thinks you're below me? I don't care much for your point of view, Connor."

My eyes were stinging, and my throat was burning, and I couldn't seem to get any words out past the giant stone lodged in my throat.

Jack rubbed wearily at his forehead. "I love you, but I can't be with someone who will always assume the worst of me. Who will never believe that I love him for who he is and that I'm not ashamed of him."

"I know you aren't," I said. "I made a stupid mistake. I am so sorry, Jack."

"You should go, Connor."

"Is this it for us?" I asked. "We're finished, just like that?"

"I don't know," Jack said. "I need some time. Can you give me that?"

I wanted to beg him to forgive me. I wanted to fall on my fucking knees and refuse to leave until I convinced Jack that I was an idiot and I'd never doubt him again.

But Jack was angry and hurt, and I knew that nothing I said tonight could convince him. I had fucked up, and I couldn't fix it. At least not right now.

"Please, Connor," Jack said. "Just go."

I almost said I loved him. It was true, and it was suddenly vital that he knew I loved him too, but it was the wrong time. He wouldn't believe me, or worse, he wouldn't care.

My shoulders slumped, and I took a deep breath. "Okay. Will you call me when you're ready to talk?"

He nodded, staring down at the island. I walked to the door and hesitated in the doorway, staring at Jack's bowed head. He didn't look up or acknowledge me, and feeling like I was making the worst mistake of my life, I walked out of his house.

CHAPTER 13

Jack

Twelve days.

That's how long it'd been since I'd talked to Connor, seen Connor, touched Connor.

I was miserable. Completely miserable.

So, call him. Please.

I stared at my phone as I sat in the parking lot of Shepherd's garage. I needed to call him, I knew I did, but despite how much I missed him, I was still upset. I wasn't angry anymore. The anger had faded quickly, but the other emotions weren't as easy to let go of. Knowing Connor believed I was just like his ex, thinking that I would ever be ashamed of him or his family, cut me to the fucking bone.

I stuffed my phone into my jacket pocket and stared out the windshield at the garage. It wasn't only Connor I missed. I missed his entire family. Dad's death had left me completely alone, and Connor's family had filled the void I felt after my parents' deaths.

I took a deep breath and climbed out of my car. Today

was Eva's birthday. I had her Barbie car in the trunk, and I was determined to give it to her, even if Connor and I were finished.

You're not finished. Just call him, you asshole!

Shepherd walked out of the garage before I had taken even a few steps from my car. Not sure what to expect, I was beyond grateful when he stuck his hand out. "Hey, Jack. How are you?"

I shook his hand as Tristan joined us. "Okay."

"Are you?" Tristan said. "You look terrible."

"Tristan," Shepherd said and cut him a look.

Tristan just shrugged. "It's true. Give me the keys to the van, and I'll bring it around front."

Shepherd handed him a set of keys as I opened the trunk and brought out the Barbie car. I'd put the car together myself last night and wrapped a giant red bow around it. I set it awkwardly on the ground. "Thanks for taking this to Eva. I really appreciate it."

"Eva's gonna shit a brick when she sees it," Shepherd said with a grin.

"Maybe you could get a video of her driving it around for me," I said.

"I'll try, but she'll probably be going too fast," Shepherd said.

I laughed, the first real one in thirteen days. "I hope she doesn't crash it on the first ride."

"Knowing her, she probably will," Shepherd said.

Tristan pulled up in a large grey van. The kind used to take ten or more people on a road trip. "You guys ready?"

"Ready?" I asked.

Shepherd clapped me on the back. "I got word of a sweet deal on a Rolls Royce Phantom. It's in rough shape, but I figured you'd probably want to look at it."

The mention of the car should have made me giddy. I'd been looking for a Phantom for years. But my car obsession didn't seem to matter anymore. Not when I didn't have Connor in my life.

So, fucking call him already!

"Thanks," I said, "but I'm pretty tired. I think I'll call it a day."

"Are you fucking shitting me?" Shepherd said. "I drop a Rolls Royce Phantom in your lap, and you're not even going to take a look at it?"

"I appreciate it, but -"

"C'mon, Jack," Tristan said, "at least look at it. It's pretty sweet. Shepherd showed me pictures of it."

"Get in the van, man," Shepherd said as he opened the side door.

"I've got candy in here," Tristan said with a grin.

I laughed again before locking my car and climbing into the van. "Yeah, okay. How far away is it?"

"Not too far," Shepherd said. "We'll bring you back here to pick up your car after we look at it."

"Okay, thanks." I settled into the first bench seat, buckling my seat belt as Shepherd slammed the side door shut. He picked up the Barbie car and loaded it into the back of the van behind the third bench seat before climbing into the passenger side.

"Drive, baby, drive," he said to Tristan.

Tristan laughed and drove out of the parking lot. Ten minutes later, he pulled into the parking lot of a coffee shop called 'The Bean Scene' and put the van in park.

I stared out the window. "The car's here?"

"Nah, we need to make a couple stops first," Shepherd said.

"For coffee?" I stared at him in confusion.

"Not quite," Shepherd said.

"What's with the van, anyway?" I asked.

The side door to the van opened, and I stared in surprise at Nora. She wore a "Bean Scene" shirt and a nametag with little coffee cup stickers plastered all over it.

"Hi, honey," she said as she climbed into the van. She pressed a kiss against my cheek before sliding onto the bench seat behind me.

"Nora? What... what are you doing here?"

Before she could reply, Angie, followed by Rob carrying two coffees, climbed into the van. She knelt on the seat beside me and cupped my face, staring intently at me. "Oh, sweetie, you look like hell."

"Angie," Nora said.

"What?" Angie kissed my cheek before moving to sit next to Nora. "He does."

"You could be politer about it."

"I don't have time for that shit." She took the coffee from Rob. "Thanks, honey."

"You're welcome," Rob said. "Hi, Jack. How are you?"

"Uh, fine," I said as Rob handed his coffee to Angie and pulled the door shut before taking the seat next to her.

Tristan pulled out of the parking lot, and I said, "What's going on?"

"Shepherd, did you see that new Netflix show yet?" Nora said. "The one about the aliens?"

"Nah," Shepherd said. "Haven't had the time. I'll try to start it next weekend."

"We watched the first two episodes last night," Angie said. "I couldn't believe when the asshole commander -"

A chorus of 'Angie, shut up!' "No spoilers!', and 'Don't you dare, Angela!" filled the van.

"All right, all right," Angie said. "Don't get your fucking panties in a bunch."

"What's going on?" I repeated as Tristan parked the van on a side street. There was a basketball court beside us full of young men shooting hoops and playing one-on-one. Shepherd stuck his head out the window and whistled piercingly.

Davey jogged off the court and climbed into the van. He fist bumped me. "Good to see you, Jack."

"You too."

"Oh my God, you're so freaking sweaty," Angie said.

"It's called exercise, Angela," Davey said as he made his way to the third bench seat. He collapsed on it with a soft sigh before looking behind him. "Sweet Barbie car."

"Oh man," Nora said as Tristan pulled back into traffic. "Eva is going to flip when she sees that thing. You're the best, Jack."

She pulled out a gummy from a small clear packet in her purse and popped it into her mouth.

"Nora, seriously?" Angie said.

"There's gonna be like a thousand kids, Angie," Nora said. "Don't tell me this isn't a smart idea."

Angie hesitated before holding out her hand. "Fuck, you're right. Gimme a gummy."

Nora handed one to her as Shepherd hollered back, "You'd better not be getting high back there."

"We're not," Nora said sweetly as she handed a gummy to Rob. She smiled at me. "I'd offer you one, but you need to be clear headed."

"Clear headed for what?" I asked. "What's happening? I thought we were looking at a car."

"We are," Shepherd said.

"Eventually," Davey said.

"May have to be tomorrow," Angie said.

"Probably tomorrow," Rob said.

I stared blankly at them. When the van stopped again, I stared at Alison and Nan standing outside of the family home with a complete lack of shock.

Shepherd hopped out of the van and opened the side door. He helped Nan into the vehicle, basically lifting her in and making her giggle like a schoolgirl. She sat next to me as Shepherd helped his mother into the van and slammed the side door.

"Hello, dearest," Nan said before patting my cheek. "I've missed you."

"I've missed you too," I said. I stared at Connor's family. "I've missed all of you."

Nora grinned at me. "Of course, you have. We're amazing."

"How is work going?" Nan said. "Mark said the other day at dinner that you were up to your eyeballs in a social media shitstorm."

"It's better now," I said. "The company's weathered the storm. Of course, it helped that we dropped the author who was a homophobic piece of crap, as well as making donations to the GLAD and The LGBT National Help Center."

"Good for you." Nan patted my cheek again. "I'm sorry that she caused such a problem."

"Me too." I could hear the bitterness in my voice. She hadn't just been a fuck up for the company, but she'd also, in a small way, been the cause of my fight with Connor. Of course, maybe it was better that I found out now that Connor would never believe I wasn't ashamed of him.

He knows that. He made a mistake. Call him.

"How is -" I stopped abruptly.

"How is who, dear?" Nan said with a small smile.

"Eva," I said. "How is Eva doing? And James?"

"Oh good, good. Eva is over the moon that it's her birthday today," Nan said. "We made her chocolate chip pancakes for breakfast, and she was so happy."

"Jack bought her the Barbie car, Mom," Alison said.

"You did?" Nan stared at me in delight. "Oh, she's going to be so excited. What a wonderful birthday gift, Jack. You're such a good boy."

She took my hand and held it tight. We lapsed into silence as Tristan drove. I had no idea what the hell was going on, but it suddenly didn't matter. Being with Connor's family made me happy, and right now, I would take all the happiness I could get.

Ten minutes later, Tristan pulled into another parking lot and shut off the van. "We're here."

I waited patiently as Shepherd helped his mother and his nan out of the van before I followed.

"Chuck E Cheese," I stared at the building in front of us. "You're taking me to Chuck E Cheese?"

"They have surprisingly good pizza," Nora said.

"Corn dogs," Davey said as he stood next to her. "I'm getting like a shit ton of those mini corn dogs. They're like crack to me."

"Shepherd," I said as we walked toward the restaurant, "you lied to me about the car?"

"No. I do have one to show you, but I set the appointment for tomorrow.:

"Okay, then why did you bring me to Chuck…"

My voice died when the restaurant door opened, and Connor, James, and Eva stepped outside. Eva's face lit up, and she sprinted across the short distance to throw herself at me.

I caught her and picked her up, smiling at her when she

kissed me on the cheek. "Jack! You came to my birthday party!"

"I wouldn't miss it for the world," I said. "Happy Birthday, kiddo."

"Thank you!" She slung her arm around my shoulders. "I'm really glad you're here. Uncle Connor's been in a bad mood ever since you stopped being boyfriend and boyfriend. He's said so many bad words that I made twenty bucks from him in one afternoon. Twenty dollars, Jack!"

"That's a lot of money," I said.

"Yep. I put it in my piggy bank for my Barbie car fund." Eva smiled again at me. "I'm seven today."

"I know."

"Bunnykins," James took Eva from me, "Uncle Connor needs to talk to Jack for a minute."

"Sure, okay. I want Jack to sit beside me at the table, okay, Daddy?" Eva was still talking a mile a minute as James carried her over to where the rest of the family stood about ten feet away.

"Hi, Jack," Connor said.

"Hi." My gaze roamed his face. He looked as tired and miserable as I felt. It didn't make me happy that he was suffering too, just depressed.

"I know I was supposed to wait for you to call me, but I couldn't wait any longer. Every day apart from you is driving me crazy."

"Me too," I said.

"I'm sorry," Connor said. "I'm so sorry for what I said. I won't say I didn't mean it because, at the time, I did, but I promise that I've realized what an idiot I am. I won't make that kind of assumption again. I know in my heart that you're not like Darryl in any way, and I regret saying that you were.

I was hurt and upset, but that isn't an excuse. I hope you can forgive me."

"I do," I said. "I forgive you, Connor."

Relief flooded his face, and the tension in his body eased a little. He reached for my hand. "Thank you. Would you be willing to give me a second chance?"

"Yes," I said. I didn't have to think twice about it. I'd missed Connor so much.

He took a deep breath and glanced at his family. "Jack, I asked my family to help me today because of two reasons. One – they care about you and want you to know that you're a part of our family now, and two – I love you. I love you so fucking much, and I want you and everyone else in my family to know it."

I swallowed hard, my eyes burning and my voice hoarse. "I love you too, Connor."

He pulled me into him for a hard kiss. I kissed him back, wishing I could take the kiss deeper, wishing I could get him naked and in my bed.

Connor pulled back a little. "We need to stop before there's an inappropriate erection situation."

I laughed a little shakily. "Yeah. I love you, Connor."

"I love you too."

Connor and I both laughed when his family started hollering and cheering. They joined us, and I was hugged and kissed and slapped on the back more times than I could count.

"You guys! You're gonna crush him. Take it down a notch," Connor said.

He took my hand, holding it firmly as Nan smiled at both of us. "You two make my heart so happy. I've got palpitations."

"I've got something for that," Nora said and passed her a gummy.

Nan popped it into her mouth before poking Shepherd in the chest. "Oh, don't give me that look, dearest. It's medicinal."

"Okay, celebrate the birthday girl's day in style," James said. "Everyone into the Chuck E Cheese. Davey, stay out of the ball pit this time, please."

As his family walked toward the restaurant, I squeezed Connor's hand and smiled at him. "Thank you."

"For what?" he said. "For being an asshole and nearly fucking everything up?"

I shook my head. "For being a man who knows when he's fucked up and apologizes for it."

Connor brushed a kiss against my lips. "I promise to never fuck up this epically again."

I laughed. "You don't have to be perfect, Connor. I love every part of you, even the parts that fuck up."

"Five dollars!" Eva hollered back at us. "You guys owe me five dollars!"

"That kid has ears like a hawk," I said to Connor.

He laughed and pulled me close as we caught up with the rest of his family. "Welcome to the Hayes family."

SEDUCE EXCERPT

SEDUCTION SERIES, BOOK ONE

Mark

I stripped off my clothes and checked the temperature of the water before stepping into the shower. I ducked my head under the hot spray, closing my eyes and doing my best not to think about how close I'd come to embarrassing the fuck out of myself in front of Dev.

My attraction to him was like nothing I'd ever felt before, but he wasn't looking for someone like me. I had no doubt that his flirting with me was nothing more than a fun game. He wasn't actually attracted to me.

You sure? Because it sure seems like he's interested in seeing you naked.

I shampooed my hair and rinsed it before lathering my body with soap. He was humouring me. The young guy taking pity on the old guy who was drooling over him.

Embarrassment made my whole body hot as I rinsed away

the soap. I might have been ashamed by my horniness for a guy half my age, but that shame didn't stop me from bracing one arm against the slick tile wall and rubbing my dick with the other. Already half hard just thinking about Dev, it didn't take long for me to grow fully erect.

I closed my eyes and jerked off with slow, long strokes, imagining it was Dev's hand on my cock, imagining his wet body pressed up against mine as he slowly, teasingly, brought me closer to my release.

My groan of pleasure cut out when the shower curtain pulled back with a rattle. I stared in disbelief at Dev as he stepped into the shower with me and pulled the curtain closed. He was naked and even in my shock, I gazed greedily at his body. Unlike my body, which was covered in a light layer of dark hair, he only had a little hair on his chest and, I swallowed hard, a neatly groomed patch of blond hair above his dick.

"I like your tattoo," he said, staring at my ribcage.

"What are you doing, Dev?" My voice was hoarse. I stood frozen with my hand wrapped around my aching cock and my gaze glued to Dev's beautiful dick.

"No hot water in my house," Dev said. "Do you mind if I use some of yours?"

He slid past without waiting for my reply, a small and cocky grin crossing his face when his ass brushed against my dick, and I moaned. He ducked under the spray, letting the water run down his perfect body before turning to face me. I told myself not to look, before staring at his dick again.

He was as hard as I was, and my hand squeezed compulsively around the base of my cock when Dev gave my dick his own long and appreciative look.

"Fuck, that's a good looking dick," he said. He licked his lips before staring up at me. "I bet you taste delicious, Mark."

I groaned and pressed back against the tile, trying desperately to maintain my control. "Dev…"

"I want to know how you taste," Dev said. "I think about it all the fucking time. I *dream* about it. What it would be like to have my lips wrapped around your cock, how you would sound as I took you deep."

I couldn't look away from Dev's gorgeous mouth. I had no idea I was pumping my dick with my hand until Dev made a noise of satisfaction. I followed his gaze to my cock, both of us staring at the plump drop of precum welling up on the tip.

I moaned when Dev swiped his thumb through it. Even that brief touch set my body aflame. Dev licked my precum from his thumb. "I was right. You taste fucking amazing."

My lust for Dev was a raging fire, a blazing heat that threatened to destroy me in the most beautiful of ways.

"I want more," Dev said.

This was wrong, so very fucking wrong, but I made no move to stop him when he crouched in front of me, his perfect lips only inches from my aching, weeping cock.

"Will you give me more, Mark?" Dev said as he stared up at me.

My free hand cupped the back of his skull and I urged him closer to my dick. "Yes, Dev, I will."

ABOUT THE AUTHOR

Evelyn Bloom writes bold and sexy M/M romances that always end in happily ever after.

When not writing, her free time consists of reading, embroidering naughty art, and watching Netflix. She has a serious addiction to lip balm, nineties boy bands, and learning curse words in other languages.

For more information about Evelyn, check out her website at

www.evelynbloom.com

facebook.com/authorevelynbloom

instagram.com/authorevelynbloom

bookbub.com/authors/evelyn-bloom

amazon.com/Evelyn-Bloom/e/B092XD2NPY

ALSO BY EVELYN BLOOM

Temptation Series

Tempt

Tease

Taste